HARRIET

'I was in the doghouse. Dad, though
outwardly calm, was clearly livid with
me. Julie and Hamish looked confused
and uncomfortable. They didn't, of
course, know exactly what had
happened, and I made no attempt to
tell them. Inwardly I was seething with
resentment at the injustice of it all.
Such a fuss over an innocent little visit
to a boy's room – anyone would think
I'd done something really shocking,
like a strip-tease in the middle of
Great School . . . '

TESSA KRAILING worked for the BBC for six years, spending most of that time in television. She then left to train as a teacher and taught for the next fourteen years in both Switzerland and England.

Tessa Krailing now devotes all her time to writing. She is the author of CINDERELLA IN BLUE JEANS (also available from Lightning).

Magic Moments

Harriet and the Hunk

Tessa Krailing

HODDER AND STOUGHTON

Copyright © 1990
by Tessa Krailing

First published in Great Britain in
1990 by Lightning

The characters and situations in
this book are entirely imaginary
and bear no relation to any real
person or actual happening.

This book is sold subject to the
condition that it shall not, by way of
trade or otherwise, be lent,
re-sold, hired out or otherwise
circulated without the publisher's
prior consent in any form of
binding or cover other than that in
which it is published and without a
similar condition including this
condition being imposed on the
subsequent purchaser.

No part of this publication may be
reproduced or transmitted in any
form or by any means,
electronically or mechanically,
including photocopying, recording
or any information storage or
retrieval system without either the
prior permission in writing from
the publisher or a licence,
permitting restricted copying. In
the United Kingdom such licences
are issued by the Copyright
Licensing Agency, 33-34 Alfred
Place, London WC1E 7DP.

Printed and bound in Great Britain
for Hodder and Stoughton
Children's Books, a division of
Hodder and Stoughton Ltd.,
Mill Road, Dunton Green,
Sevenoaks, Kent, TN13 2YA.
(Editorial Office: 47 Bedford
Square, London WC1B 3DP)
by Cox & Wyman Ltd.,
Reading.
Photoset by Chippendale Type,
Otley, West Yorkshire.

British Library C.I.P.

Krailing, Tessa, *1935–*
Harriet and the hunk.
I. Title II. Series
823'.914 [F]

ISBN 0-340-51794-8

One

'Hey, Harriet – come and look at this!' Julie dragged me over to the fifth-year notice board.

INTERSCHOOL TRIVIA QUIZ
We shall be looking for two team members to represent Bradley High School in the forthcoming Trivia Quiz, sponsored by the Bradley Chamber of Commerce, to be held in the Town Hall on Saturday, 11 February. If you're interested let your tutor know.

'You should enter,' she said, when I'd had time to read it.

'What's the point, Julie? I'm only a fifth year. They're bound to choose sixthformers.'

'No, they're not. They wouldn't have put it on our notice-board if they didn't want fifth years to go in for it.'

I stared at the notice. It's true that I'm good at general knowledge. Or, to put it another way, I have a gift for collecting useless information. My mother says I store up facts the way a squirrel hoards nuts.

I've also had plenty of practice at quizzes. Dad and I play Trivial Pursuit pretty well every weekend and the score works out fairly even. He's good on Science and Nature; but I can beat him hollow on Art and Literature and Entertainment.

Neither of us is much good on Sport.

'I expect St Olav's will be competing,' Julie said. 'They're bound to put up a strong team.'

St Olav's was the boys' boarding school where my father taught. They were our chief competitors at everything from soccer matches to chess.

Steve Harris came up to read the notice over my shoulder. Julie said to him, 'I'm trying to persuade Harriet to put her name down.'

Steve grinned. 'Certainly the Owl should enter. It'll give her the perfect chance to show off her incredible brain power.'

Julie glared at him, as if she was the one who'd been insulted. In fact I don't give a hang about people calling me the Owl: since I have to wear spectacles I reckon I may as well wear them good and large, so in a way I ask for it. I grinned back and said, 'Hadn't you better run along and mug up your two times table, Cloth Ears? We've a Maths test later.'

As we walked away down the corridor Julie muttered, 'Don't take any notice. He's just jealous because you're smarter than he is.'

'I suppose you realise,' I said gloomily, 'that if I do get selected for this quiz team it won't improve my chances of being asked out on a date? Boys hate girls to be smart.'

'Only the thickos. What you need is to meet somebody who's intellectually your equal. Then you'd click straight away.'

Julie is a born romantic. 'It's all very well for

6

you.' I cast a jaundiced look at her honey-blonde hair and small, curvy figure. 'You click with just about every boy you meet. But as soon as I hove over the horizon they run a mile.'

'That's only because they're scared of you.'

'*Only*! What am I – some kind of Frankenstein's monster?'

'Don't fish, Harriet,' Julie said sternly. 'You know very well that you've a lot going for you in the looks department. Your hair's a lovely chestnut colour and your eyes are nice when you take off those horrendous spectacles. And you have beautiful teeth.'

'All the better to eat up little boys,' I said, gnashing them.

'Anyway, looks aren't important. It's personality that counts – and you've plenty of that.' She added thoughtfully, 'If anything, a little too much. Perhaps that's the trouble.'

I stared at her. 'In what way, too much?'

'You are inclined to be forceful.'

'I don't suffer fools gladly, if that's what you mean.'

She looked doubtful. 'Most people are foolish about something, you know. Someone who's brilliant at Maths can be hopeless when it comes to mending a fuse. There are different kinds of intelligence.'

'I can mend a fuse,' I said, immediately on the defensive. 'My mother taught me.'

We had arrived outside the classroom door. Our next lesson was French, never one of my favourites. Despite my ability to remember facts, I didn't

7

exactly shine at anything academic. My only real talent was for Art, but even that was inclined to be quirky, by which I mean that I loved drawing rather odd-looking people but couldn't work up the least bit of enthusiasm for landscape or still life.

As we entered the classroom Julie murmured, 'Anyway, you will, won't you?'

'Will what?'

'Enter for the quiz.'

'I'll think about it,' I said.

I thought about it, on and off, for the rest of the day. I was still thinking about it as I walked home along Byron Avenue and turned into the drive of our house.

Dad's car, an ageing Ford Cortina, was parked outside the garage, but this didn't mean he was back yet. Most days he cycled. Because St Olav's was a boarding school he had to work late nearly every evening, supervising prep and doing dormitory duty.

As I walked up the drive I saw a pair of track-suited legs sticking out from under the car. 'Hi, Hamish,' I said, stepping over them.

A muffled grunt was the only reply.

Hamish McDermid was one of Dad's tutees. He seemed to spend most of his spare time over at our house these days, tinkering with the Cortina. Not that you really noticed he was around. He was one of those large, silent types.

Mum was in the kitchen, peeling the packaging off a frozen pizza. 'Hello, Harriet,' she said when she saw me. 'Good day at school?'

'So-so. How was yours?'

'Don't ask!'

She teaches the reception class at the local primary school, and always comes home pooped. Mind you, I'm not surprised. I went there once, as part of a community project, and it nearly blew my mind. Twenty-nine infants with runny noses and droopy drawers, all demanding non-stop attention – it was enough to make anyone head for the nearest padded cell. If I were an infant teacher I'd tie them to their chairs and shove outsize lollies in their mouths to keep them quiet.

Mum put the pizza into the microwave. 'Give Hamish a call, will you? I expect he's hungry.'

'He's always hungry.' I opened the kitchen window and yelled 'Hamish!' at the top of my voice, then turned back to ask, 'What about Rupert?'

'He's watching a cartoon. It'll be over in a minute.'

My ten-year-old brother is a telly addict. He's hooked on everything from She-Ra to cookery programmes. The way he abuses his eyesight he should be the one who has to wear spectacles, not me.

I helped myself to some apple juice from the fridge. 'Mum, do you think I'm too forceful?'

She looked surprised. 'I wasn't aware of it. Except, I suppose, we're all a bit on the forceful side. We're that kind of a family.'

I knew what she meant. We were all inclined to speak our minds, which sometimes led to fierce arguments. But we were none of us prone to the sulks, or to harbouring grudges. I couldn't bear to belong to a family where people didn't speak to each other for days.

'Who said you were forceful?' Mum asked.

'Julie. She said I scared boys off.'

'If they scare that easily they're not worth bothering about.' She plonked a bowl of salad in the middle of the table. 'Let's ask Hamish. Hamish, are you scared of Harriet?'

I turned to see Hamish standing in the doorway. He looked so startled by Mum's question that I wanted to laugh. The idea of a hulk like Hamish being scared of anyone was frankly comic. Six feet of solid muscle, with shoulders like an American football player, he could steamroller any opponent into the ground.

'Don't answer that question,' I said quickly, to save his embarrassment. And mine.

'No, perhaps you'd better not.' Mum smiled at him. 'Come and sit down.'

Without speaking, he held out his hands. They were black with oil.

'You'll find the Swarfega in the cupboard under the sink,' she said. 'No, on second thoughts, you'd better let Harriet get it for you. Otherwise you'll leave black fingerprints all over the paintwork.'

He grinned at her sheepishly. I took out the jar of Swarfega and handed it to him. He muttered, 'Thanks,' and started rubbing the liquid into his hands. His arms were bare – he had on an oil-streaked T-shirt – and I couldn't help noticing how brown and muscly they were, like a grown man's. It occurred to me that some girls might find him attractive, because he did have very nice eyes – grey, with little black flecks in them – and naturally wavy brown hair. Personally, I've always preferred brains to brawn.

I asked him, 'Hamish, did you hear about this inter-school quiz that's being sponsored by the Chamber of Commerce?'

'Aye, we were told about it yesterday.' His Scottish accent, although not broad, made everything he said sound crisp and definite.

'Will St Olav's be entering a team, do you think?'

He rinsed his hands and dried them. 'Sure to.'

'Any idea who they'll choose?'

Hamish thought for a minute. His thinking processes were inclined to be slow. You could almost see the little cogs going round in his brain. At last he said, 'Well, J.J. Dexter for one. They're bound to choose him.'

I'd heard of J.J. Dexter. He was St Olav's high flyer, intellectually speaking, brilliant at Physics and Chemistry. Dad said he was almost certain to get a top scholarship to Oxford.

I'd also seen him, although only from a distance, when Dad took us along to special occasions such as Speech Day and the school play. He *looked* brainy somehow, with straight dark hair that flopped over his forehead and a thin, clever, thoughtful kind of face.

Competing with J.J. Dexter would be a real challenge . . .

'What quiz is this?' Mum asked as we sat down at the table.

'It said "trivia" on the noticeboard,' I told her. 'I

imagine that means the kind of questions you get in Trivial Pursuit. As a matter of fact, I'm thinking—'

Before I could finish my brother Rupert erupted into the room and threw himself on to a chair. 'Oh, gosh, pizza, great! I'm starving.'

'Hands,' Mum said sternly.

He groaned and went over to the sink.

'Go on, Harriet. You were saying something about the quiz . . . '

'Only that Julie said I ought to go in for it. I might not get chosen, of course, but they seem to be encouraging Fifth Years to enter as well as Sixthformers, so it might be worth trying. And if it's going to be trivia type questions I should stand a good chance.'

'Yes, you should,' Mum agreed. 'Heavens knows you've had plenty of practice.'

Rupert dried his hands and sat down at the table. 'If you want my opinion, Harriet should definitely go in for it. She's such a smartypants, she's sure to win.' He started sawing up his slice of pizza. 'And even if she doesn't she'll have a fantastic time showing off, you know what she's like.'

I glared at him. 'Of course, *you* never show off?'

'Not the way you do, no.'

'How about the time you played a ghost in the school play and kept appearing on the castle battlements when you weren't supposed to?'

'I was getting laughs,' he said smugly. 'The audience loved me.'

'You're just a ham actor. It comes from watching too much television.'

12

'I'd rather be a ham actor than a knowall.'

'Square Eyes!' I snapped.

'Four Eyes!' he retorted.

'Oh, for goodness sake belt up, the pair of you.' Mum turned to Hamish, who was meanwhile tucking into his pizza. 'Do you have any brothers and sisters, Hamish?'

'Aye,' he said, chewing methodically. 'One brother, one sister. Both younger than me.'

'And are they as argumentative as this at mealtimes?'

'I wouldn't know, Mrs Bowles. I hardly ever see them. They live with my mother in Canada.'

We turned to stare at him.

'My parents split up.' He sounded quite unconcerned about it.

'Oh, I see,' Mum said. 'So that's why you're at boarding school?'

Hamish nodded. 'I spend most of the time with my father, but he has to travel a lot because of his job. If he's away during the holidays I have to stay with my aunt. She lives in Aberdeen.'

St Olav's, I thought, must be the nearest thing to a permanent base that he has. It made me suddenly appreciative of my own united family. Rupert could be infuriating at times, but I'd hate to be separated from him if Mum and Dad went off in different directions.

This was such a sobering thought it made me quiet for the rest of the meal, which was so unusual that Mum inquired if I was feeling okay.

When we'd finished Hamish went back to the car and Rupert to the television. 'Poor Hamish,' I

13

said as Mum and I washed up the dishes. 'I didn't know his parents were divorced.'

'Neither did I,' she said grimly. 'If I had I wouldn't have put my big foot in it the way I did. Really, your father is too bad. I wish he'd fill me in with some of the background details of the boys he invites to the house.'

'Perhaps he didn't think it was important?'

'Well, he *should* think! If his mind weren't so cluttered up with bits of useless knowledge he might be able to sort out what's really important for a change.'

This was a dig not only at Dad, but at me as well. Mum had no patience with our passion for Trivial Pursuit. She said it was a terrible time-waster and she'd sooner read a good book any day.

After a while I wandered out to where Hamish was working on Dad's car. He had the bonnet up and was leaning over, fiddling with a tappet or a grommet or whatever it is people fiddle with in engines. I said, 'Hamish, about this quiz . . . do you really think J.J. Dexter will go in for it?'

Hamish grunted something without looking up, which I took to be yes.

'But does he have a good general knowledge?' I persisted. 'I mean, he might be brilliant at Physics and Chemistry but not have a clue about pop music or Charles Dickens or World War II. It's the *breadth* of your knowledge that counts in a trivia quiz.'

Hamish muttered something under his breath. When I asked him to repeat it he straightened and said, 'Breadth, not depth.'

14

Surprised, I demanded, 'What do you mean by that?'

He shrugged. 'Quizzes only test superficial knowledge. J.J. may refuse to have anything to do with it. He'll probably think it's beneath him.'

'*Beneath* him?' My voice was squeaky with indignation. 'He should be proud to be chosen. *I* shall be proud, if I'm lucky enough to get on the team.'

Hamish gave me a sideways, measuring look. I had the feeling he didn't altogether approve of me, and this gave me an uneasy jolt.

Or maybe it was just quizzes he didn't approve of?

I asked abruptly, 'What does J.J. stand for, anyway?'

'No idea. Everyone calls him J.J., I've never heard him called anything else.'

'What's he like? As a person, I mean.'

Hamish shrugged. 'He's okay. Bit of a loner, goes around in a dream most of the time. Useless at sport.'

Definitely my type of person. I'm useless at sport too. I remembered Julie saying, *What you need is to meet somebody who's intellectually your equal. Then you'd click straight away.*

J.J. Dexter would be my equal, if not my superior. If I couldn't click with him, then I was unlikely to click with anybody. This threw a whole new light on the Interschool Trivia Quiz and made it more desirable than ever that I should be chosen for the High School team.

Not only desirable. Essential.

I said to Hamish, 'Tell J.J. he has to enter. Tell him it will be to his advantage and may even change his life.'

He stared at me as if I'd gone stark, raving mad.

Two

Julie was waiting for me outside the Sixth Form Library. 'You've been in there ages,' she said as soon as I emerged. 'Did you get selected?'

Twelve of us had put our names down for the quiz team, two fifth years and the rest sixthformers. First we'd had to complete a written paper, and then the best six had been asked to take part in a sort of dummy run so that the final four could be chosen. It had been a pretty nerve-racking experience. I came out of the Library feeling as if my legs were made of cotton wool.

'Well?' Julie prompted.

'Yes, I got selected,' I croaked. 'But I'm not sure now that it was such a good idea.'

'Why ever not?'

'It was awful. Everything I knew seemed to go out of my head. I felt so stupid.'

'You couldn't have been that stupid or you wouldn't have been chosen.'

We started to walk down the corridor, back to our own fifth year area. 'I didn't think I'd be so nervous,' I said, still shaking like a leaf. 'Things don't usually affect me that way. I don't know what came over me.'

'Maybe it's because you wanted it so much,'

Julie said. 'You were really keen to be on the team, weren't you?'

'Yes, I was.' I groaned. 'And that was only the dummy run! What on earth am I going to be like when it comes to the real thing?'

'Don't start worrying about it yet, for heaven's sake. You've plenty of time to get yourself psyched up before then – ten days at least.'

We'd reached the coffee bar. I sank on to the nearest stool and Julie went off to get me a reviving coffee. While I was waiting Steve Harris came by and asked how I'd got on. 'Fine,' I said, trying to sound off-hand. 'The questions weren't too bad. Quite easy, in fact.'

'Oh well, they would be, wouldn't they? I mean, Harriet the Owl finds everything easy.' Grinning, he bent nearer to whisper, 'I came across a poem the other day. It starts off, "Girls who wear spectacles, Never get their necks tickled . . . "'

'Ogden Nash,' I snapped. '1860 – 1934.'

I'm good on dates of birth and death.

Steve laughed. 'Best of luck, anyway,' he said, and wandered off.

He hadn't meant to be malicious, I knew that. It was just his warped sense of humour. I comforted myself with the thought that J.J. Dexter would never make jokes about spectacles: he'd probably recognise them as a sign of intellectual superiority and be more interested in girls who wore them than in girls who didn't. Who wants their necks tickled anyway?

Julie came back with two coffees and said, 'You

didn't tell me who else got selected. Were you the only fifth year?'

I nodded. 'From the sixth form there's Clare Myers and Colin Butcher and Harvey Feldman. Harvey's good, but his brain works so fast he can hardly get his tongue around the answers. Clare and Colin are okay on their pet subjects, but they don't have all that wide a knowledge. I don't know if we'll be strong enough to beat St Olav's.'

Julie frowned. 'It's not really the sort of thing you can practise for, is it, because you don't have a clue what questions are likely to come up?'

'No,' I agreed. 'But it scared me today how nearly I went to pieces under quiz conditions. I can at least prepare myself better for that.'

'How?'

'By getting someone to fire questions at me, against the clock. Julie, are you doing anything this weekend?'

'I'm going to a disco tomorrow night with Mark Foster. Otherwise nothing special.'

'In that case could you come over to my house in the morning and test me? I've got some quiz books we could use.'

'Okay. Yes, I'd like to.'

'Thanks.' I smiled at her and sipped my coffee. It was my intention now to train as hard as I could for the inter-school quiz at Bradley Town Hall. The last thing I wanted to do was show myself up for a first-class idiot in front of J.J. Dexter.

Dad was late home that evening so I didn't have a chance to tell him I'd been selected until breakfast next morning. Of course he pretended he'd known all along that I would be, but I could tell he was secretly delighted by the way he pulled at his beard and creased up his baggy eyes. (Dad has a lot of bags under his eyes, but they're not all due to overwork: Mum swears he was born with them.)

'You will come, won't you?' I asked him anxiously.

'A horde of stampeding buffalo couldn't keep me away.'

'But who will you be rooting for – Bradley High or St Olav's?'

'Both,' he said. 'If either team gets into the final I shall be chuffed to dollrags.'

This gave me a bit of a jolt. I'd almost forgotten there'd be other schools competing. The way I saw the final, there'd be just two people in the spotlight, me and J.J. Dexter, locked in a spine-tingling confrontation.

'Dad,' I said, 'has St Olav's chosen its team yet?'

'Ah.' He tapped the side of his nose mysteriously. 'Now that comes under the heading of classified information. I'm not sure I can tell you.'

'Oh, don't be so maddening! Are they having a dummy run, the way we did?'

'Nothing so organised. The Head Man's passed the whole thing over to a member of staff, and left it up to him to make the final decision.'

'Which member of staff?'

'Me.'

I nearly threw my bowl of cereal at him.

'No doubt the Head Man knows you're an

acknowledged expert on quizzes,' Mum said drily, pouring him a second cup of tea. 'To say nothing of the fact that he was probably keen to offload the responsibility on to someone else.'

Dad grinned. 'You could be right – on both counts.'

(In case you're wondering why Rupert took no part in this conversation, I should explain that we have a portable TV on the kitchen dresser and he was therefore glued to Breakfast Television, despite the fact that Mum insisted he watched it with the volume turned right down.)

'So who,' I persisted, 'are you going to choose?'

'Two from the Upper Sixth, I expect, and two from the Lower.'

'Who from the Lower?'

He shrugged. 'Could be Johnson and Clarke.'

My heart did a lurch. 'What about J.J. Dexter?'

'Mmm, well . . . I'm not sure about Dexter. He may not have the right temperament.'

'How d'you mean?'

'He's primarily a scholar. That means he's good at written work, but not particularly quick-witted verbally. He needs time to think.'

I was beginning to like the sound of him more and more. A deep thinker was just the sort of person I could admire. I said persuasively, 'You could at least give him a try.'

'Perhaps I should,' Dad agreed. 'Especially as he's inclined to be jealous of his status with the rest of his year and might well be disappointed if he were passed over.'

'Which suggests he must have a competitive spirit,' Mum said.

'That's true.' Dad glanced at his watch and drained his cup. 'I must be off. Some of us have to work on Saturday mornings, you know.'

Mum gave him her sweetest smile. 'We *all* have to work on Saturday mornings, dear. When else do you think the washing and ironing and shopping and hoovering gets done?'

He grinned, unrepentant, and bent to kiss her goodbye. In passing he ruffled Rupert's hair and patted me on the shoulder, then stopped in the doorway to say, 'By the way, I told young Hamish he could come over this morning to change my sump oil. He can't make it this afternoon because he's playing in the House rugger match.'

'Talking of Hamish,' Mum began, 'I do think you might have told me about his parents —'

But it was already too late. Dad had gone.

He's just *got* to choose J.J. for the team, I thought, closing my eyes and willing him to make the right decision.

'Headache?' Mum inquired solicitously.

'A bit of one,' I lied, opening my eyes again. 'Mum, I've asked Julie over this morning. She's going to test me for the quiz.'

Mum sighed. 'That means, I suppose, that you won't be available to help me with the chores? And I can't use the car to go shopping, because Hamish will be underneath it, draining off the sump oil. Sometimes I get the distinct impression that Fate is conspiring against me.'

'Perhaps Fate's trying to tell you that you

should put your feet up,' I suggested, 'and let everything go hang for once.'

'Don't tempt me!' She got to her feet and started clearing the dishes. As she took away Rupert's plate she passed a hand in front of his eyes, but his trance-like stare remained fixed on the TV screen. 'What's more, my son seems to have turned into a zombie. Tell me, Harriet, since you know all the answers, where did I go wrong?'

Her words stung a bit. I was well aware that I didn't know all the answers, not where Life with a capital L was concerned. I wasn't even sure I knew the questions.

When Julie arrived we went upstairs to my room. I gave her one of my quiz books and a stopwatch I'd borrowed from Dad's desk. He used it for coaching athletics in the summer – about the only kind of sport he enjoyed. 'Skip the easy ones,' I told her. 'Make them as difficult as you can.'

'They all look pretty difficult to me,' she said.

'I mean the ones like which is the longest river in the world. Or the highest mountain. Or the fastest animal. They're the sort of goofy questions everyone knows the answer to.'

'I don't.'

'You must do. Now start the watch and see how many I can answer in one minute.'

She started the watch. 'Who wrote *Great Expectations*?'

'Charles Dickens. Too easy.'

'Okay, so what Polish astronomer discovered in 1512 that the Sun is the centre of the solar system?'

'Galileo. Still too easy.'

'Oh, yes? Well, you happen to be wrong. It was Copernicus.'

I smote my forehead with my fist. 'Of course! Galileo was Dutch. Ask me another.'

'What are the natives of Tangier called?'

I thought for a moment and giggled. 'Tangerines?'

'Yes!'

'Really? I only said it as a joke. Go on.'

She asked me ten questions within the minute and I managed to answer five of them correctly. We tried again, several times, but my score remained more or less the same, only a fifty-per-cent success rate. I began to feel depressed.

'I don't know what you're so worried about,' Julie said. 'I couldn't answer any of them. You must have the most amazing memory.'

'Dad says it's photographic,' I said shortly. 'Let's try again.'

'No, you're getting tired. I think we should take a break.'

'Okay.' I flung myself back on the bed and rubbed my eyes. The imaginary headache I'd told Mum I had earlier was fast becoming a reality.

Julie wandered around the room, looking at the photos I'd Blu-tacked to the wall. They weren't just rock stars: I'd cut out pictures of everyone I admired, from Beethoven to Mother Teresa. 'Who on earth's this one?' she demanded.

I raised my head from the pillow. 'Henri of Navarre. He used to be King of France.'

'I'll say this for you, Harriet. You're certainly different.'

The way she said it made it clear that by "different" she actually meant "eccentric". I supposed she was right, in a way: I'd never gone for the obvious heroes that everyone else has.

'Now *that*,' Julie went on, 'is definitely my type!'

'Which one are you looking at?' I raised my head again.

She was standing by the window, gazing down at our driveway. 'The boy who's working on your father's car. He's the most gorgeous hunk I've ever seen.'

'Oh, you mean Hamish.' I flopped back. 'You wouldn't really like him, not if you knew him. He's terribly dim.'

'He doesn't look dim. And he has lovely muscles.'

'Honestly, Julie! You can't judge the contents of a parcel by its packaging, you know.'

'With packaging like that,' she murmured, 'who cares about the contents?'

Not for the first time I realised that in some essential respects Julie and I weren't a bit alike. She always fell for the big, beefy types, like Mark Foster whom she was going to the disco with tonight. Brains didn't actually count for much with her.

I said loftily, '*I* care about the contents. Muscles can wither and sag. The more muscular a man is when he's young the flabbier he's likely to get when he's older. It's what a person's like inside that matters, because that's the part that lasts.'

Julie wasn't even listening. 'Introduce me,' she said.

'Now?'

'Yes, please.' She turned to the door.

'But we're supposed to be practising for the quiz . . . '

'Oh, hang the quiz. I want to meet him.'

I sighed and got off the bed. 'Okay. But don't blame me if you're disappointed.'

Hamish was just closing the car bonnet when we arrived downstairs. 'Hi,' I said to him. 'Finished already?'

'Aye, it's not a long job.' His gaze travelled past me to Julie and widened somewhat. She had that effect on boys.

'This is my friend Julie Summers,' I said, trying to disguise the fact that I found this whole situation rather embarrassing. I hoped he wouldn't guess the real reason for our sudden appearance and hurried on, 'She's been testing me for the quiz.'

'Oh, I see.' He turned away to wipe his hands on a rag.

'Harriet's brilliant at quizzes,' Julie put in. 'Did you know she's been selected for our team?'

He shook his head.

'I'm useless when it comes to general knowledge,' she informed him with a frank smile. 'Are you any good at quizzes, Hamish?'

I said quickly, 'Hamish is better at sport. He's playing in the rugby match this afternoon for his House.'

'Oh, I *love* watching rugby.' This was an outright

26

lie: Julie hated standing out on cold pitches in an icy wind just as much as I did. But she flapped her eyelashes at Hamish and purred, 'It's such an exciting game. Much more exciting than soccer, I think.'

Hamish stared at her.

Meanwhile my brain had gone into overdrive. I suddenly saw this afternoon's rugger match as a heaven-sent opportunity for me to bump into J.J. Dexter, accidentally on purpose. Okay, so he was unlikely to be a spectator, being the non-sportive type, but to get to the playing fields we'd have to walk through the school quadrangle . . .

'Why don't we go along and watch?' I suggested to Julie. 'We could cheer on Hamish's House. I'm sure they'd be glad of our support.'

'Oh, that's a fantastic idea!' She turned to me with a look brimful of gratitude and enthusiasm. 'Harriet, you're a genius.'

'Yes, I know,' I said caustically. 'Okay, Hamish, you can expect to see us on the sidelines. What time does the match start?'

'Two-fifteen,' he said, looking a little stunned.

'Great! We'll be there.'

Three

'Absolute genius!' Julie kept muttering as we walked from the bus stop up the long tree-lined drive that led to St Olav's. 'You must have been inspired, Harriet.'

I didn't deny it.

'I don't think it's genius,' Rupert grumbled, lagging slightly behind us. 'If you ask me, this is a lunatic idea.'

When Mum heard we were going to the match she'd insisted we took Rupert, to get him out in the fresh air and away from the dreaded Box. I didn't raise any objections, mainly because I thought that having a boy with us would look less suspicious than two girls on their own. With luck people would assume it was Rupert who'd wanted to come and he'd dragged Julie and me along to keep him company.

We reached the grey stone building that was the main part of the school and walked through the archway into the upper quadrangle. St Olav's had originally been built as an abbey, so the quad was enclosed by cloisters where the monks used to walk. Now it was inhabited by racing, rowdy, preoccupied-looking boys – but not one of them was J.J. Dexter. I walked as slowly as I could, my eyes on swivels, until Julie urged me to hurry.

We passed under a second archway and came out on the path leading down to the playing fields. My disappointment was intense. I don't know quite what I'd hoped would happen – at least a sighting, I suppose; at best a close encounter. But looking for J.J. was like looking for some rare, elusive bird.

'There's quite a crowd,' Julie said when we arrived at the rugger pitch. 'Who'd have thought so many spectators would turn up on an afternoon like this?'

I should have mentioned, it was a bitterly cold February day with the wind blowing straight from the North Pole. Julie and I were both wearing denims and padded jackets zipped up to our chins. She had pulled her hood over her head, which on her looked quite glamorous, but if I'd done the same I'd have looked like Dracula's mother, so instead I wore a white woollen hat that covered my ears. As for Rupert, he had on so many sweaters that if you pushed him over he'd have rolled around like a beer barrel.

To my relief, there were several other girls shivering on the touchline. St Olav's had recently gone co-ed in a half-hearted sort of way, taking in a few females at sixth-form level. Dad had vaguely hinted it might be possible for me to make the transition if I wanted, but I'd said no thanks, I'd sooner stay at Bradley High.

Now I wasn't so sure. If J.J. Dexter and I should happen to click . . .

'Here come the teams,' Julie said, nudging me in the ribs. 'I can see Hamish. Wow, he's got the most fabulous legs!'

30

Cheered by their supporters, the players charged on to the pitch like gladiators entering the Roman arena, full of brash self-confidence. Hamish, looking large as a house and about as immovable, was unmistakeably the leader of his team. The legs Julie so much admired were brown and sinewy as tree trunks.

'He has an amazing tan, considering it's February,' she drooled. 'But I suppose that's because he's the outdoor type. He probably keeps it topped up all the year round.'

'For heaven's sake,' I muttered, 'do try to restrain yourself a little, especially *devant* the *enfant*.' I jerked my head at Rupert.

'Oh, don't mind me,' he said with a sigh. 'Just tell me how long we've got to stick this out, that's all. Can we go home at half-time?'

'Stop whinging, Rupe. You watch rugger for hours on television, so why not the real thing for a change? After all, you don't get the proper atmosphere at home.'

'You don't get pneumonia either,' he pointed out. 'And you have a commentator to tell you what the rules are.'

'We already know what the rules are.'

'I don't,' said Julie.

'Well, you should do,' I said sternly. 'You're the one who told Hamish you enjoyed watching it.'

She shot me a surprised look. 'Why are you so bad-tempered, Harriet?'

'I'm not,' I snapped, stamping my feet. 'I'm just cold, that's all.'

And fed up, I added mentally, *at not seeing J.J. Dexter*.

Once the game started, though, I had to admit that Rupert might be right about preferring to watch it on television. It's a very physical game, rugby. On television you don't hear the grunts and sickening thuds as the players cannon into each other or hit the ground. It began to remind me even more of the Roman arena, with the crowd yelling for blood, and it surprised me that Hamish, who'd always seemed rather a gentle giant, should appear to enjoy it so much. At one point he did a flying tackle only a little way from us, bringing down his opponent. Immediately five other boys threw themselves on top and there was a horrendous scuffle.

Eventually the scrum parted to reveal Hamish lying flat on his face in the mud. As he struggled to his feet Julie yelled, 'Give it to 'em, Hamish!'

Still swaying, he glanced in our direction and blinked. Then, without a flicker of recognition, he stooped to pull up his socks and ran off.

'He looked straight at us!' Julie said triumphantly. 'Harriet, do you think he knew it was me?'

I shrugged. 'Hard to tell. I guess his mind was on other things.'

'My mind's on other things too,' Rupert grumbled. 'Like hot buttered toast and tomato soup and—'

'Are my eyes deceiving me?' Dad's voice came from behind us. 'Or is this actually my unsporting family I see before me?'

We hadn't seen him since breakfast, so he

couldn't possibly have known we were coming. I felt a bit embarrassed, especially when he went on, 'What on earth's come over everyone? Has the television broken down – or did your mother throw you out of the house?'

'Something like that,' Rupert said grimly.

'Anyway, what are *you* doing here, Dad?' I demanded. 'You're no more sporting than we are.'

'It just so happens that I'm senior tutor to Burton House. Burton are playing, therefore I'm honour bound to come and support them. That's the rule with house matches. Everyone has to stay for at least the first half.' He said "Hello" to Julie and took up a position between Rupert and me, hugging his arms against the cold. 'What's the score?'

None of us had a clue.

'That's what I like,' he said. 'Informed spectatorship.' Raising his voice he asked the same question of a boy further along the touchline, who told him it was 9–6 in Burton's favour. After a few minutes of pretending an avid interest in the game, he said to me in a low voice, 'By the way, I took your advice.'

My mind was blank. 'What advice was that?'

'About the quiz. I had a chat with J.J. Dexter this morning. Seems he's quite keen on the idea. Mind you,' he added, 'you may wish you'd never suggested it. He has a pretty sharp brain.'

'All the better,' I said, trying not to show how delighted I was. 'It'll make the competition more interesting.'

'Mmm. Well, you should be able to give him a

run for his money.' Dad suddenly raised his voice to yell, 'Come on, Burton! What are you waiting for?'

When he'd quietened down again I asked, 'Dad, what sort of questions is he best at? Apart from science, I mean.'

Dad shrugged. 'Why don't you ask him? He's standing just over there, on the other side of Julie.'

I was stunned. How could I have been standing so close to J.J. Dexter all this time without being aware of it? But I'd been so certain he wouldn't be at the match I hadn't even bothered to look, forgetting that he'd have been press-ganged into supporting his House, like everyone else in Burton. I leaned forward slightly to look past Julie, trying not to be too obvious.

Yes, he was there all right. But it was no wonder I hadn't recognised him. His blue-and-white St Olav's scarf was wound several times around his neck and covered most of his face, leaving only his nose and a pair of dark, miserable eyes visible over the top. All that showed of his skin looked chalk-white against the familiar lock of straight black hair.

My heart did the most incredible plunge, right down to the heels of my waterproof boots.

'Go on,' Dad urged. 'Have a word with him, why don't you?'

'I – I don't like to.'

'Harriet Bowles, don't tell me you're shy!'

'No, of course not,' I growled defensively. 'But he doesn't know who I am. He'll think it odd . . . '

'Oh, for heaven's sake!' Before I could stop him Dad had reached behind me to tap J.J. on the shoulder. 'Dexter, I don't think you've met my daughter Harriet? She'll be competing against you in the inter-school trivia quiz I told you about this morning, for Bradley High.'

J.J. glanced at me vaguely, as if he hadn't a clue what Dad was talking about.

'Hi,' I said, with an over-bright smile, secretly cursing Dad for landing me in this situation. It seemed so false, somehow, and not at all how I'd imagined our first meeting. 'Are you looking forward to it?'

His expression, what little I could see of it, remained blank.

'The competition, I mean.'

'Oh. Yes, moderately.'

Dad had faded away, back to his place on the touchline, leaving me stranded. Desperately trying to sound casual, I burbled, 'I suppose Science is your best subject? Mine's Literature, but I'm not bad on Entertainment, especially old black-and-white movies. I adore those. In fact they're the only things I really enjoy on television. How about you?'

'I don't care much for television.' His voice, muffled by the scarf, was light and rather clipped. 'Most of the programmes are moronic rubbish. Watching them's a criminal waste of time.'

'I agree,' I said quickly. 'Especially the quizzes. They're usually far too easy. Except for Youth Challenge – I quite like that one. It's more intelligent than most, don't you think?'

'I've never seen it.'

'Oh.'

End of conversation. I searched my mind frantically for a new topic, but before I could think of one Julie gripped my arm.

'Harriet, Hamish is hurt!'

I looked where she was pointing. There'd obviously been an incident on the far side of the pitch, judging by the crowd that had gathered. Then I saw that Julie was right – a couple of Burton boys were helping a limping, mud-spattered Hamish over to the touchline where someone was waiting with a sponge.

'He was kicked,' Julie said indignantly. 'I saw it happen. One of the other team lashed out with his foot just as Hamish was passing. He did it on purpose, I'm sure he did.'

'Barbarous game,' J.J. commented beside me.

'Absolutely,' I agreed.

'It's a mystery to me why anyone should want to spend their time running around a field and getting covered in mud – with the sole object, apparently, of trying to kick an oblong ball between two white posts. I mean, what is the point?'

'I don't think there is one,' I said, with a scornful little laugh.

The referee blew his whistle.

'Half-time,' J.J. said with relief. 'Now we can escape this torture.'

He turned on his heel and started walking away.

Julie stared after him. 'Who on earth was that pompous twit?' she demanded.

'J.J. Dexter,' I replied. 'And he isn't pompous, just very, very bright.' I started to follow him.

Julie grabbed my arm. 'Where are you going?'

'It's half-time. Everyone's leaving.'

'But what about Hamish? I thought we'd come to watch him play. We can't leave now.'

I shook her off. With every second of delay J.J. was getting farther and farther away. 'I've had enough. Come on.'

'Harriet!' She grabbed me again. 'We could at least make sure that Hamish is okay.'

From behind us Dad said, 'Just what I'm proposing to do. You can come with me, if you like.'

Inwardly I groaned. J.J. was already too far ahead: I'd never catch him up now. 'Okay,' I said reluctantly. 'Then we'll go home.'

Rupert cheered.

When we reached the crowd around Hamish, Dad pushed in and Julie went with him, but I hung back. After a few minutes she emerged looking rather straight-faced and said, 'He's all right. We can go now.'

'What's the matter?' I hurried after her. 'Wasn't he pleased to see you?'

She didn't answer.

We left the field, Rupert in tow, and walked up to the quadrangle. No doubt about it, I could tell from her set expression that something had annoyed her. Maybe Hamish hadn't realised who she was?

My suspicions increased during the bus-ride

home when she did nothing but talk about going to the disco that evening with Mark Foster. In a way it made me feel better about not having clicked with J.J. Dexter. After all, if a girl like Julie failed to make an impact at first meeting, it didn't seem so surprising if I couldn't manage it either. These things took time, I told myself.

And in exactly one week I'd be meeting J.J. again – as his opponent in the inter-school trivia quiz.

Four

Next day – Sunday – Hamish came over to our house in the afternoon. There wasn't any work to be done on the car, but Dad said he could give it a wash-and-polish if he liked. My own private guess was that Hamish was bored at school and didn't know what else to do with himself.

About four o'clock Mum suggested I made some tea. I took hers and Dad's into the living-room, with a glass of milk for Rupert, and stuck my head out of the window to give Hamish a call. When he came into the kitchen I handed him a mug and asked if his leg was okay.

'Fine,' he said, eyeing the plate of brownies Mum had taken out of the oven about half-an-hour ago.

I offered him one. 'Julie – that's the friend who came with me yesterday – was quite worried about you. She said the other boy kicked you on purpose.'

Hamish, biting into the brownie, only shrugged.

'I don't know how you can enjoy playing rugger,' I went on. 'It's such a barbarous game.'

I loved that word 'barbarous'. It was so clever of J.J. to use it. Most people would have said 'barbaric', which I supposed meant roughly the same thing; but 'barbarous' sounded far more intellectual.

Hamish said, 'It gets rid of surplus energy. People of our age have a lot of surplus energy. They've got to burn it up somehow.'

'But it's so *aggressive*. That's why it surprises me that you enjoy it. I wouldn't have said that you were a naturally aggressive person.'

He reached for another brownie. 'That's because I get rid of all my aggression on the rugger pitch.'

'But surely there must be other ways of getting rid of it, without actually hurting people?'

'Plenty,' he agreed. 'You can ride a bike – or take up jogging – or knock the living daylights out of a punch-ball. It doesn't really matter what you do, as long as you take some form of exercise. At least, that's my opinion.'

All physical pursuits, I noticed. 'What about mental exercise?' I challenged. 'Isn't it more constructive to channel one's surplus energy into that?'

Hamish shrugged. 'Depends on your temperament, I suppose.'

I was glad that my temperament – and J.J.'s – was strictly of the mental variety.

Casually I announced, 'I met J.J. Dexter yesterday. He was watching the match as well.'

'Oh, aye?' Hamish sounded guarded.

'He's definitely going to be in St Olav's team for the quiz. It's been decided.'

'That's good.'

'Good for you, maybe,' I said with a show of

modesty. 'I'm not so sure about us. He seems pretty bright.'

Hamish said, rather dubiously, 'Bright at some things, maybe. But not everything.'

I felt myself bristling on J.J.'s behalf. 'What do you mean – not everything?'

'He can be a little short on commonsense.'

'A quiz isn't meant to test your commonsense,' I said tartly. 'It tests your brains.'

'Oh, well . . . ' Hamish drained his mug and set it on the draining-board. 'J.J. has plenty of those.' He went to the door. 'I'd better get on with the polishing. Thanks for the tea.'

As the door closed behind him I pulled a face. Clearly Hamish had no patience with brainy people; he'd think far more highly of J.J. if he clumped around the rugger pitch with the rest of them, getting covered with mud. Typical macho attitude. I washed up his tea mug and went back into the living-room.

'I can't think why that boy spends so much time at our place,' I muttered, flinging myself into a chair. 'Surely he could find something better to do with his time?'

'Hamish?' Mum glanced up from her book. Sunday afternoon was her sacred time for reading. 'I think he likes being with a family. After all, he doesn't have one of his own – at least, not a proper one.'

'But he hardly sees us,' I pointed out. 'He spends all his time under Dad's car.'

'It's the car he comes to be with,' Dad agreed. 'He's far more interested in engines than people.'

41

'That's nonsense,' Mum said. 'Really, Colin, you can be incredibly dense at times.'

He grinned at her. 'You're just a little old sentimentalist at heart. I know how boys think – heck, I spend all my life with them, don't I? – and I promise you, Hamish doesn't have any hang-ups about his parents' divorce. He's just a normal red-blooded bloke, good at games, average at work, one of the most popular boys in the school. The only reason he likes coming here is that I let him tinker with my car to his heart's content. It's as simple as that.'

Mum gave him a frosty look and went back to reading her book.

During the following week at school Julie was full of her date with Mark Foster and didn't once mention Hamish. If I hadn't known her better I might have put this down to extreme fickleness of nature, but I guessed she was probably still smarting from whatever insult, real or imagined, he must have dealt her. However, I didn't lose any sleep over it. I was too busy being kept awake by my own worries about next Saturday. These were, in ascending order of magnitude:

a) What if I couldn't answer *any* of the questions and had to pass on every one?

b) What if, on account of my stupidity, Bradley High failed even to get through the first round?

c) What if J.J. forgot that he and I had met on the rugger field and completely ignored me?

There were other minor anxieties, most of them related in some way or other to the aforesaid major ones, with the result that by Saturday I was practically a nervous wreck.

The Bradley High team met at school immediately after lunch – I hadn't been able to eat a thing – and were taken to the Town Hall in the school minibus, driven by the deputy Head, Mrs Castellani.

As the minibus crawled through the streets of Bradley, jammed with Saturday afternoon shoppers, Colin Butcher asked, 'Do we know how many schools are competing?'

Colin was almost as nervous as I was, I could tell by the way his trouser legs were shaking.

'Four,' Mrs Castellani replied. 'That means there'll be two rounds, and the winners of the first round will compete against each other in the final.'

'If we're drawn against St Olav's in the first we're sure to get knocked out right away,' Colin said gloomily.

'Don't be so defeatist.' Mrs Castellani tooted at two women carrying on a conversation in the middle of a zebra crossing. 'We're perfectly capable of beating St Olav's, as long as you all keep your heads.'

'Luck comes into it too,' Clare Myers pointed out. 'A lot depends on the kind of questions we're asked.'

'Don't forget we have a secret weapon,' Harvey Feldman said.

We all looked at him questioningly.

'Harriet's glasses.' He shot me a fiendish grin.

43

'When the other teams see those they'll be so dazzled they won't dare open their mouths.'

'Oh, ha, ha!' I said with heavy sarcasm, getting in quickly before anyone else had a chance. 'You're a fine one to talk, Harvey Feldman. Just wait till they catch sight of your teeth.'

Harvey had very large white teeth which stuck out in front, like a rabbit's. When the others laughed he looked furious and Mrs Castellani said, 'I think you'd better quieten down now. We're just about to arrive.'

But laughter had broken the tension and everyone was in a far more relaxed frame of mind as the minibus drew up outside Bradley Town Hall.

We were welcomed by a man called Tom Byford, the councillor whose idea it had been to hold the quiz and who was to act as quizmaster. He was large and cheerful-looking and I liked him immediately. He took us into one of the committee rooms to meet the other teams and prepare for the quiz.

St Olav's were the last to arrive – Dad's fault, he'd mistaken the time – and I saw J.J. the minute he entered the room. He didn't look too happy, I thought. Perhaps he was feeling nervous too?

I edged closer, and under cover of the general hubbub, managed to say, 'Hi. I'm Harriet Bowles, your tutor's daughter. Remember me?' Which was a kind of insurance, just in case he didn't.

He gave me a surprised look. 'Of course I remember you. We only met last Saturday.'

I couldn't make up my mind whether this was

44

hopeful or not. But before we could say anything more Tom Byford called for silence so that he could explain the rules.

The contest would be divided into two parts. First each member of the team got a solo turn, answering questions on the subject of his or her choice. Then there'd be a free-for-all to test our general knowledge, the first person to press the buzzer getting the chance to answer.

The draw to decide which schools played each other had already been made. We were to go first, against the Convent. As Mrs Castellani ushered us out of the room I glanced back over my shoulder, hoping that J.J. might at least wish me good luck, but he was staring out of the window.

By this time quite a crowd had gathered in the hall where the quiz was to take place. I could see Mum in the fifth row with Rupert on one side of her and – to my amazement – Hamish on the other. I wouldn't have thought this was his scene at all, but decided he must have been commanded to come and support St Olav's. By accident or design, I wasn't sure which, Julie was sitting right behind him, with some other kids from Bradley High.

As we took our places on the dais my stomach was churning over like mad, but the moment the quiz began I forgot about feeling nervous and started to enjoy myself. For my solo round I chose Art and Literature. My score was high and so was Harvey's on Science and Nature. But when it came to the general questions I got really carried away, hitting the buzzer first nearly every time

45

and getting the answers out fast. We won easily, 46 to 27.

By now I was on an all-time high. It was frustrating to have to wait around while St Olav's played their first round match against Bridge Street Comprehensive, but of course I had to watch, to see how J.J. made out. He was brilliant on his chosen subject – Science and Nature – and got the maximum score possible; but on the general questions he was slow to buzz, even when he obviously knew the answer. St Olav's won, but it was a much closer contest than ours.

After that came the tea break. Or, as Dad put it, the statutory bunfight. Mum and Rupert came over to congratulate me, with Hamish tagging along behind, and seconds later Julie arrived, bursting with enthusiasm. 'You were great, Harriet! Absolutely brilliant. You'll beat St Olav's easily.' This was said in a much louder voice than normal and with much flashing of her eyes, which made me suspect she was putting on a show for Hamish's benefit, even though she hadn't so much as glanced in his direction.

'Don't start counting chickens,' I warned her. 'It's by no means a foregone conclusion.'

'But you're so quick! Isn't she quick?' Julie turned to appeal to the others, her gaze skating rapidly over Hamish. 'Honestly, Harriet, I don't know how you manage to keep so cool under that kind of pressure. I'd go completely to pieces, I know I would. You must have nerves of steel.'

Rupert said, 'She's not quite human, didn't you

know? Bradley's one-and-only walking encyclo-paedia.'

Julie laughed. 'You could be right!'

By chance I happened to look at Hamish just in time to see a flicker of a grin cross his face, although it went as soon as he caught my eye. This annoyed me a little. Worse, it sowed a seed of doubt in my mind, totally undermining my confidence.

Could it be that boys really regarded smart girls as a bit of a joke?

And if so, did "boys" include J.J. Dexter?

"Scuse me,' I muttered, setting my empty cup down on the nearest trestle table. 'I have to speak to someone.'

J.J. was standing slightly apart from the rest of St Olav's crowd, thoughtfully munching an almond slice. I approached, looking as casual as I could; then gave an exaggerated start as if I'd only just recognised him.

'Oh, hello,' I said. 'What did you think of the questions?'

He shrugged. 'Fairly predictable, on the whole.'

Anyone else would have said something like 'okay' or 'not bad'. I was filled with admiration.

'Have you played Trivial Pursuit before?' I inquired.

'Once or twice.'

'Dad and I play nearly every weekend. He says it helps to sharpen up his wits.'

He glanced across at my father, who was talking to Tom Byford. 'Mr Bowles has a very quick brain. I wouldn't have thought he needed to sharpen it up by playing games.'

Something in his tone – a hint of condescension in the way he said 'playing games' – made me ask, 'Don't you approve of quizzes?'

'Not entirely. They're hardly a test of one's intelligence, are they? The kind of knowledge they deal in is purely superficial.'

'That's what Hamish said,' I admitted. 'He said you probably wouldn't even want to be on the team. You'd think it beneath you.'

'Hamish McDermid?' He sounded surprised. When I nodded he said, 'Well, he was right. I didn't want to, not at first. But your father talked me into it.'

Good old Dad. I said, 'Anyway, you're not sorry now, are you? I mean, it's only for fun. You don't have to take it too seriously.'

J.J. considered this statement. Then he said, 'Oh, but I think you do. I think you should take everything seriously. Now I've entered I want to win.'

St Olav's, I noticed, didn't come into it: he was looking for a personal triumph, rather than the victory of his school.

But then, to be honest, wasn't I too secretly hoping to get more than my fair share of the glory if Bradley High were to win? We were two of a kind, J.J. and me, both natural competitors.

'It's odd there are no girls in your team,' I remarked, 'considering you now have some in the Sixth Form. Is there some reason for that?'

J.J. looked blank. 'I've no idea. You'll have to ask your father.'

As if on cue Dad chose that moment to come

up behind us. He put an arm around my shoulder and gave me a squeeze. 'Well done, Harriet.' He grinned across at J.J. 'Now for the second round – the battle of the Titans, eh?'

I wasn't sure whether he meant St Olav's versus Bradley High – or J.J. versus me. But as we filed back on the dais for the final I found myself in the grip of a terrible dilemma.

Should I go flat out to win the contest for Bradley High?

Or would I make a better impression on J.J. Dexter if I held back and let him have his personal triumph?

Five

I didn't, of course. When it came to the final I couldn't stop myself from trying every bit as hard as I'd tried in the first round and my score was equally high. Not that it made any difference. St Olav's won by 42 to 36.

The problem was that both Harvey and J.J. wanted to answer questions on Science and Nature, but according to the rules once somebody had chosen a subject it was no longer available for the other team. St Olav's won the toss; therefore J.J. had first choice and poor old Harvey had to opt for Geography, which he didn't like nearly so well.

J.J. was fantastic. He dropped only one point and even that made him furious with himself. During his round I sat gazing at him with rapt admiration, thinking how intelligent he looked, and falling deeper and deeper into a state of besottedness.

This did not, however, affect my own performance in the free-for-all. I was still faster on the buzzer than anyone else and beat J.J. several times to a question he could have answered just as easily I did. Afterwards I wished I hadn't, but by then it was too late. In the committee room afterwards I searched anxiously for him, intending to apologise, but Dad had whisked the St Olav team away as soon as the competition was over. So instead I went to commiserate with Harvey, who was in a very glum mood.

It was while we were chatting together that Tom Byford came over to murmur comforting platitudes like, 'That was a close-run thing,' and 'It's a pity somebody has to lose on these occasions.' Then he took me aside and said, 'Your father tells me you really enjoy this kind of contest, Harriet?'

I had to admit that I did. 'Of course I know it only tests one's superficial knowledge, but – yes, I do enjoy it.'

'I'm glad to hear that, because — .' He broke off and winked mysteriously. 'Well, I'd better say no more for the moment, except I've another idea up my sleeve that may interest you. I need to make some enquiries, but if things turn out according to plan I'll be in touch.'

I hadn't a clue what he was talking about, so I smiled vaguely and promptly forgot all about it.

When Dad came home that evening I asked if any of the Sixth Form girls had wanted to be considered for the team and he said no, they'd shown no interest. It wasn't really their scene.

Which made me more certain than ever that I'd made a serious blunder in trying so hard to compete with J.J. Dexter.

On the other hand, if I hadn't entered for the quiz I'd never have got to meet him at all.

I went to bed in a state of confusion and tossed and turned all night, asking myself imaginary questions that were impossible to answer. But the real conundrum was, *How on earth was I ever going to meet J.J. again, now that the quiz was over?*

Next day Hamish came to Sunday lunch, at Mum's invitation. It was clear she now regarded it as her mission in life to provide him with a proper home environment, with us as his surrogate family. As he sat chomping away at his roast beef and Yorkshire pudding I asked him, 'Did you celebrate last night?'

He stopped chomping to look at me inquiringly.

'St Olav's victory in the quiz. Did you celebrate?'

'J.J. was cheered in the dormitory before Lights Out,' he said. 'He seemed rather embarrassed about it.'

I liked this suggestion of modesty. Hungry for any information I could get about my beloved, I asked, 'Do you think it's changed his mind about quizzes? Will he be keener to take part in them in future?'

Hamish shrugged. 'I shouldn't think so. He said this was definitely a one-off.'

'Sensible boy,' Mum remarked. 'If he's hoping to get a scholarship he'll have to put his time to more constructive use, not fritter it away on trivialities.' She caught my eye and added, 'Sorry, Harriet, but it's the truth.'

'Some people make a lot of money out of going in for quizzes,' Rupert pointed out. 'TV quizzes and game shows often have fantastic prizes. If you're clever you can practically make a living at it.'

Dad raised an eyebrow. 'And is that what you're proposing to do?'

'I might,' Rupert said offhandedly. 'Harriet's not the only one around here with brains, you know.'

'Saints preserve us!' Mum said with a long-suffering sigh.

When we'd finished eating Hamish muttered something to Dad about checking the car's exhaust system, but before Dad could answer Mum said, 'Oh no, Hamish, not today. You're here as our guest, not as a motor mechanic. In fact I thought we could all do something together this afternoon.'

Dad stared at her. 'Such as what?'

'Such as going for a walk.' She added defiantly, 'It's a nice, brisk afternoon. A walk will do us good. As a family, we don't take nearly enough exercise.'

Rupert looked aghast. I said quickly, 'I take plenty of exercise. At school we get gym twice a week *and* compulsory games.'

Dad said, 'What about me? I cycle to and from work every day.'

'And Hamish certainly doesn't need it,' I pointed out. 'He's a rugby player.'

'Stop quibbling.' Mum got up from the table and wound an apron round her waist. 'As soon as we've washed up we'll get the car out of the garage and drive up to Wych Cross. From there we can take a good long walk over the heath. Get some fresh air into our lungs.' She started clearing the dishes. 'Come on, Harriet, give me a hand.'

When the others had gone I said, 'Okay, Mum, so where's the ulterior motive?'

She put on an air of surprised innocence. 'What makes you think I have one?'

'Come off it! You hate walking just as much as the rest of us. No, my guess is that it has something to do with Hamish, since he's your Good Cause of the moment – although how on earth taking him on a forced march across Bradley Heath is supposed to help him is beyond me.'

Mum smiled. 'All right, I'll come clean. The idea is to give us a chance to draw him out – make him talk about himself and his family. It's always easier to talk when you're walking. At least one of us should manage to break through the barriers he puts up.'

'I don't think he puts up barriers,' I said. 'At least, not intentionally. He's just naturally reserved.'

'Nobody's naturally reserved. People get that way when they're left alone too much and turn in on themselves. All he needs is someone to show a little interest in him – someone who cares.'

'He's a games-player, Mum. Dad says he's one of the most popular boys in the school. If he's reserved with us it's because we're not really his kind of people. We're not sporting enough. Honestly, if you'd seen him on the rugger pitch you wouldn't feel sorry for him. He's tough as old leather.'

She sighed. 'You're as bad as your father, only judging by appearances.'

I didn't bother to argue. I was convinced I was right.

Yet, on the drive to Wych Cross, squashed between Hamish and Rupert in the back seat, I couldn't help being intrigued by his silent presence beside me. Did anything go on inside his brain, apart from car maintenance and rugger tactics? Was he, in fact, just a good looking hunk – or could there be more to him than that?

Dad parked the car in the National Trust car park. Bradley Heath was designated "an area of outstanding natural beauty" and it certainly lived up to its name today, bathed in the pale golden light of a winter sun. Even for a family of notoriously reluctant walkers like ourselves there was a kind of exhilaration in stretching our legs over the high rolling heathland.

Mum went ahead with Hamish while Dad, Rupert and I followed on behind. She looked quite small beside him and had to walk fast to keep up with his long, athletic strides. I could see her asking him questions, but it seemed as though his answers were slow in coming – and pretty short when they did come. I suspected she wasn't making much headway.

Dad and I amused ourselves by testing each other on how many plants we could name, while Rupert did nothing but grumble because he was missing the Sunday afternoon film. When we reached the highest point on the heath, known as Didbury Beacon, we stopped and dutifully admired the view.

'They say you can see four counties from up here,' Mum said.

'Fancy!' Dad's tone was ironic.

'Your trouble is that you have no soul,' she complained.

'Oh yes, I have,' he said. 'But it's not the kind that finds fulfilment in pastoral scenes. The fact is it'd be far happier at home with the Sunday Times crossword.'

'Well, your soul may not appreciate the exercise,' Mum said tartly, 'but your heart and lungs will certainly be grateful. Look at the way you're all puffing and panting.'

This was true. The final climb up to the Beacon had left most of us somewhat short of breath.

'Hamish is the only one who's really fit,' she declared. 'All right, I give in. Let's go home.'

Somehow, I don't quite know how, I found myself walking with Hamish on the way back, with Mum and Dad ahead of us and Rupert some distance behind. Remembering what Mum had said about drawing him out, I drew his attention to the heather and asked if he'd spent much time in Scotland.

'Quite a bit,' he said. 'When I was younger.'

'I thought you must have done, because of your accent. I suppose that's where your home was, before — ' I stopped myself just in time from saying 'before your parents were divorced' and substituted – 'before you came to St Olav's?'

He nodded. 'Near Aberdeen.'

'Oh, that's where your aunt lives – the one you have to go and stay with in the holidays if your father's abroad.'

He looked puzzled. 'How did you know that?'

'You told us, don't you remember? It sounded

57

as if you didn't like going there much. Is she difficult?'

'No, she's okay. But she's my great-aunt really, so she's pretty old. I prefer being with my father.'

I wanted to ask why he'd chosen to stay in this country when his brother and sister went to Canada with his mother, but couldn't think of a tactful way of putting it. Instead I asked, 'Where does your father live when he's not travelling?'

'He has a flat in London, near Victoria station.'

'That must be handy when you have to catch a train.'

'Yes, it is.'

Heck, I was making an awful hash of this! I burbled on, 'Do you mind being at boarding school? I mean, some people hate it, don't they? But I suppose if you're good at games it isn't so bad. People who are good at games are usually popular – much more popular than the studious ones. J.J. Dexter, for instance – does he have many friends?' I hadn't meant to talk about J.J., but the question just popped out.

'Not many,' Hamish replied. 'I think he prefers books to people.'

'Oh, so do I,' I said fervently. 'Although I do have a few friends. But some people think I'm rather eccentric – because of my glasses, I suppose – so they tend to leave me alone.'

After a pause Hamish said, 'I like your glasses.'

'Do you?' I felt myself flushing. I'm not good at accepting compliments. 'Thanks.'

'You wouldn't be you without them.'

'No. Well, I did think about contact lenses, but

58

apparently I've the wrong kind of eyesight. So I'm stuck with these.'

We lapsed into silence. I was annoyed with myself for letting the conversation drift away from Hamish's problems to J.J.'s and then mine. But while I was trying to think of a way to steer it back on course Hamish suddenly said, 'There's a dance next month at St Olav's.'

This came as no surprise. There was always a dance at St Olav's towards the end of the spring term. They invited the girls from the Convent and it was a very starchy affair, with the staff from both schools turning out in force to make sure there was no hanky-panky behind the bike sheds. I'd never been, but Dad had us weeping tears of laughter when he described the event. The result, he said, was usually a nil-nil draw, thanks to mafia-like surveillance.

Hamish went on, 'I was wondering if you'd like to come?'

For a moment I thought I'd misheard him. Or if not misheard, certainly misunderstood. 'With you?' I asked stupidly. 'As your partner?'

'That's right.'

I glanced at him sideways, but he was staring straight ahead, his face empty of any expression. 'What – what about the girls from the Convent?' I stammered.

'There aren't usually enough to go round. That's why we're allowed to bring our own, if we want.'

'Oh, I see.' The words were automatic, masking the frantic activity in my brain. Surely this was the answer to my prayer? If I went to the dance with Hamish there'd be a good chance I'd meet up again with J.J. Perhaps attendance at the dance was compulsory, like rugby matches, if only for the first half? I might even get to dance with him . . .

But it would hardly be fair to Hamish, to accept his invitation as a way of getting to see J.J. I wasn't sure I could be so unscrupulous as that.

And then there was Julie . . .

I cleared my throat. 'Could I bring a friend with me? The truth is I'd be a bit scared to come on my own. Anyway, if you're short of girls you'd probably be glad of one extra.'

He turned to stare at me. 'I wouldn't have thought you'd be scared, Harriet. I didn't think you were afraid of anything.'

'Well, you're wrong,' I said, a little more sharply than I intended. 'I'm petrified of social occasions, especially dances. In fact I never go to them if I can help it.' I saw the bewilderment on his face and hastily added, 'But I'd like to go to this one, especially if I could bring Julie with me. You've already met her – she's the friend who came to the rugger match.'

'I remember. Pretty girl, with blonde hair.' He looked thoughtful. 'Yes, why not? She can be Dave's partner.'

'Who's Dave?'

'Dave Wilcox. He's a nice bloke, but rather shy.'

Like you, I almost said. But then I realised this wouldn't be true. As I'd said to Mum, Hamish was reserved, but that wasn't the same thing as being shy. He was silent from choice, not because he was tongue-tied.

'Okay,' I said. 'I'll ask her tomorrow, at school. By the way, when is it?'

'Saturday, 4th March.'

Less than three weeks away. I didn't feel too guilty now about saying yes, because my conscience was appeased by the fact that the invitation included Julie. This would give her a second chance with Hamish, who'd probably fall for her heavily when he saw how well she could dance, leaving me free to go off in pursuit of J.J.

Brilliant! I spent the rest of the walk talking quite easily to Hamish, not about his family but about all sorts of other things, from music to politics. To be truthful, I did most of the talking, but it wasn't altogether one-sided.

Later, when we got home, Mum said, 'You and Hamish seemed to be getting along rather well, I thought. Did you find out anything more about his family?'

'No, I gave up trying,' I said. 'How about you?'

She shook her head. 'He seems reluctant to talk about them. I had hoped he'd find it easier to unburden to someone of his own age.'

'Well, he didn't.' I paused for effect. 'But he *has* invited me to the St Olav dance.'

'No!' She looked amazed. 'Are you going?'

'Yes, of course.'

She looked even more amazed. 'But you hate dancing!'

'Used to.' Grinning, I picked up a kitchen chair and started to waltz around with it. 'I think I may be about to change my mind.'

Six

Next day at school I told Julie about the St Olav dance on 4th March. She said doubtfully, 'I think that's the date my cousin's having a party.'

'But this is a *dance*, Julie! And at St Olav's.'

She shrugged. 'From what I've heard, their dances are nothing to write home about. Dead old-fashioned.'

'You'll get to meet Hamish again,' I pointed out.

'Big deal!' she said scornfully.

'But I thought you liked him? You said he was the most gorgeous hunk you'd ever seen.'

'And *you* said he was dim. What's more you were right.'

I frowned. 'Julie, what exactly happened at that rugger match? When you went to see if he'd hurt himself, I mean. Did he say something rude to you – something that's put you right off him?'

'Not rude exactly.' She evaded my eyes. 'He just didn't know who I was, that's all.'

'He was in agony at the time,' I reminded her. 'Anyway, he knows who you are now. He said you were pretty.'

Her eyes widened. 'He did?'

'Yes. And he wants you to come.'

'He actually asked for me – as his partner?'

'Well . . . ' I hesitated, reluctant to tell an out-right lie. 'There'd be the two of them – Hamish and his friend Dave. We'd be a sort of foursome. But I expect you'd end up with Hamish – in fact I'm sure you would.'

If things went according to plan, I added silently.

'Oh well, that's different,' Julie's eyes lit up. 'I can wear my new dress – the one Dad bought me for my birthday. You know – I showed it to you . . . '

'You mean the red taffeta with the bow on one shoulder?'

'That's it. I don't often get the chance to wear it, but the St Olav's dance is just the right sort of occasion. How about you?'

'Don't know yet. I haven't thought.'

'Will you buy something specially?'

'Shouldn't think so. Can't afford it.'

'Perhaps your mother could make you one?'

'She loathes dressmaking.'

Julie sighed. She knew as well as I did that I had absolutely nothing suitable in my wardrobe to wear to the St Olav dance. I loathed posh frocks. They didn't suit me at all. Put me in frills and I looked like a performing monkey.

'In that case,' she said, 'you'll have to make it yourself. You're artistic – you should be good at dressmaking.'

'I wouldn't know about that. I've never tried.'

'Don't worry. I'll help you.' Her face took on a crusading look. She loved getting to grips with other people's problems. 'There's a load of pattern

64

books in the Home Economics room. We'll browse through them during break.'

But none of the dresses in the pattern books was being worn by my type of person. 'It's the specs,' I grumbled. 'When's the last time you saw a fashion model wearing glasses? Glasses and *haute couture* just don't mix.'

'Then leave them off,' Julie suggested callously.

'I can't. I wouldn't be able to see a thing.'

'You won't need to. The lights will be turned down so low your glasses won't make any difference.'

'Not at a St Olav's dance. Dad says they leave the lights full on all the time, in case people try to sneak off together.'

Julie groaned. 'Look, here's a section called "*Individualiste*". That sounds hopeful. You're definitely an individualist, Harriet.' She started flipping through the pages.

'There!' I stabbed my finger at a girl in a mauve dress with a flared skirt that dipped to the ankles at the back and rose above knee-length in front. 'How about that one?'

Julie stared at it dubiously. 'It's a bit . . . funky.'

'I like the style.'

The truth was that the girl in the mauve dress looked more like me than any of the other drawings. She didn't wear spectacles, of course, but her hair was straight and brown like mine, and she had a jaunty, slightly defiant expression that said, "Look out, world, here I come!"

'Well, at least it's marked "easy/*facile*", Julie

said resignedly. 'We'd better go straight into town after school and see if Lansdowne's stock it.'

Lansdowne's had the pattern all right, but it was exorbitantly priced. I couldn't believe they had the nerve to charge so much for a few pieces of tatty loo paper, but the woman said loftily that it was an exclusive design. I said that at that price it had better be!

'Now to choose the material,' Julie said as we turned away from the counter. 'I think it would look best made up in a sort of slinky jersey-knit . . . '

'Don't be daft,' I growled. 'I can't possibly afford to buy material after paying so much for the pattern.'

'But surely your parents — ?'

'They're both schoolteachers,' I reminded her. 'And last week our mortgage repayments went up. I'd prefer not to ask.'

'So what are you going to do?' she demanded. 'Wear the actual pattern? That should create a sensation.'

'No, I'll have to make do with what I can find at home. We've a trunk full of old curtains and things in the attic. I'll go up there tonight and take a look.'

As we left the store Julie cast a backward, wistful glance at the lengths of jersey-knit tempt-ingly draped over the stands.

The trunk yielded a stack of cast-off curtains in beige folk-weave and floral-patterned dralon – not exactly what I had in mind. There was also, however, a selection of ancient bedspreads which had become redundant when the Bowles family went over, *en masse*, to using duvets. Among these was one that used to be Mum and Dad's, in a sort of sexy sea-green watered-silk type of material. I held it against myself in the attic and it hung beautifully.

When I asked Mum if I could have it she looked dubious and said, 'Yes, of course . . . but wouldn't you rather we bought something?'

'No, thanks,' I said firmly. 'This is ideal.'

'And you're sure you want to make it yourself . . . ?'

'Quite sure. Julie's going to help me. She's coming round on Saturday so we can start cutting it out. Will it be okay if we use the kitchen table?'

'I suppose so. You'd better give it a good scrub first, though, or you'll end up with marmalade over everything.'

I'll bet Zandra Rhodes never has these problems, I thought.

When Julie saw the material she said, rather grudgingly, 'It has possibilities, I suppose. Okay, let's start by sorting out the pattern pieces.'

We had everything spread out on the kitchen table, and were poring over the complicated pattern, when the back door opened and Hamish walked in.

'Don't look!' I shrieked, trying to block his view. 'You're not allowed to.'

'Why not?' He peered over my shoulder. 'What are you doing?'

'It's a secret. Go away.'

'But I want to wash my hands.'

He'd found more work to do on Dad's car, heaven knows what. 'You'll have to use the downstairs cloakroom,' I said. 'You can't come in here.'

Julie said, 'We're making a dress for Harriet to wear to the dance.'

'Oh, I see.' He looked at her gravely. 'You're coming too, I hear?'

'Yes, I am.'

'I'm glad.'

'So am I.'

Of all the inane conversations! Suddenly impatient, I pushed him out of the door.

Julie said reproachfully, 'You might have let him in.'

'Are you mad? Didn't you see how dirty he was? He could have touched something vital, then we'd have had to start all over again.'

'But you made an awful fuss. Anyone would think you were a bride on her wedding day, not wanting the groom to see her dress in case it was bad luck.' Julie gave me a hard look. 'Are you *sure* you don't fancy him yourself?'

'Positive.'

She turned back to the table. 'Then you must be blind, that's all I can say.'

'It's cruel,' I said, 'to mock a person's disability.'

'Harriet! I didn't mean — ' She saw I was joking and threw a piece of screwed-up pattern paper at me. 'Oh, you're impossible! Come on, let's try and finish the cutting-out.'

In fact we managed to finish not only the cutting-out but also the pinning-up that first Saturday. I spent the following week tacking the pieces together and next weekend went over to Julie's, so that we could use her mother's sewing machine. The dress was beginning to take shape. Privately I thought it promised to be pretty sensational.

We made some mistakes, of course. I tacked one set of darts inside out and it took us ages to get the sleeves right. But the real revelation to me was how much I enjoyed doing it. I'd hated sewing at school, but this was different. Even though we were working to a pattern there was something creative about it that I found deeply satisfying. I couldn't wait to see the finished product.

On the morning of the dance I awoke with a thumping headache and cramps in my stomach. After lunch I threw up and Mum suggested I went to lie down for a bit. 'You don't think I'm sickening for something?' I asked her anxiously.

'No, I don't,' she said. 'But you've been working too hard on that dress and now you're overtired. Take it easy for an hour or so and you'll feel fine.'

I did as she suggested but it only made things worse. I kept having these waking nightmares, such as all the seams on my dress coming undone just as I was about to dance with J.J. The look on his face as I stood there in my bra and panties, with a mass of sea-green material draped around my feet, made me break out in a cold sweat.

Even worse was the dream where he brought a partner, a terribly intellectual girl who was actually his cousin, and they'd been practically engaged, he told me, since they were both in their prams . . .

'Harriet!' Dad called from downstairs. 'Can you spare a minute? I've something to tell you.'

I heaved myself off the bed, pulled on my dressing-gown, and staggered down the stairs.

'You okay?' he inquired when he saw me. 'Your mother says you're not feeling too good?'

'No, I'm not. I think maybe it was something I ate.'

'Sounds more like nerves,' he said. 'I expect you're getting yourself all screwed up about tonight. Never mind, I've some news that'll take your mind right off it. Come into the living-room and I'll tell you.'

Rupert was there, watching a Laurel & Hardy film. He moaned when Dad switched it off, but Dad said, 'Shut up and listen. This is a lot more exciting than old knockabout movies.'

I perched on the arm of a chair. My stomach was still churning around like nobody's business and I couldn't imagine anything would be exciting enough to take my mind off tonight. Dad simply didn't appreciate what was at stake.

'Tom Byford called me today,' he said. 'He wants to put forward your name, Harriet, for Youth Challenge.'

'Youth Challenge?' I repeated stupidly. 'Another quiz, you mean?'

'Not just another quiz, no. *The* quiz.'

'The television quiz?' squeaked Rupert. 'He wants Harriet to go on *television*?'

'That's right!' Dad looked at me, positively glowing with triumph. 'It seems she made quite an impression on him during the inter-school trivia contest. He says that's what gave him the idea that Bradley should enter a team for next year's series, so he wrote off to the BBC for details. Apparently they hold auditions all over the country during the next couple of months, so he has to get the application in fairly quickly. Well, what do you think?'

I was too stunned to think at all.

'She'll be famous!' Rupert stared at me, goggle-eyed. 'I'll have a sister who's been on TV.'

'Harriet?' Dad prompted.

'It – it wouldn't be . . . just me, would it?' I asked nervously.

'No, of course not. Every town has to enter a team consisting of a boy and a girl, you know that. Tom wants Bradley to be represented by you and J.J. Dexter.'

I swallowed hard. 'Me – and J.J.?'

'Well, you were the two who did best on the trivia quiz, so obviously you're first choice. If J.J. won't do it I suppose he'll ask Harvey Feldman.'

'You think J.J. won't do it?'

'No idea until I ask him.'

'Tonight,' I croaked. 'Will you ask him tonight?'

'At the dance?' Dad pulled at his beard. 'I could do. In fact it might be a good opportunity, with the two of you there together. But I expect he'll want to go away and think about it.' He gave me a hard look. 'How about you? You haven't said yet whether *you* want to do it.'

'I'll do it,' I said. 'Provided J.J. says yes.'

'But not if it's Harvey?'

'No.'

'You surprise me,' Dad said. 'I'd have thought you'd jump at the chance, no matter who else was chosen.'

I said evasively, 'I'd feel safer if J.J. was the other team member. He knows more than Harvey.'

For a moment Dad looked puzzled, then he shrugged it off. 'Oh well, we'll just have to wait and see what J.J. decides tonight. Then I'll call Tom Byford tomorrow and give him our answer.' He got to his feet. 'I must go and tell your mother.'

When he'd left the room Rupert muttered deliriously, 'I can't believe it – one of our family on television!'

'Don't get too carried away,' I warned. 'I have to get through the audition first.'

He wasn't listening. 'You'll probably meet Terry Wogan. And Bob Monkhouse and Esther Rantzen . . . '

I stood up, pulling the ties of my dressing-gown tighter. 'It's time I got ready. Julie will be here in an hour.'

It wasn't until I was halfway up the stairs that I realised my headache had gone and my stomach had returned to normal. In fact I felt fine. You'd think it would be the opposite, after hearing about the quiz, but Dad was right – his news had taken my mind right off the dance.

What's more, I now had the perfect excuse for seeking out J.J. – namely, to persuade him that he and I were the only two possible people to represent Bradley Town on television.

Seven

We decided it would be more fun if Julie brought her stuff in a suitcase over to my house, so we could get ready for the dance together. Then Dad would take us both in the car to St Olav's, since he had to be there anyway, on surveillance duty.

Julie and I took ages over making ourselves look spectacular. We zipped each other into our dresses and did each other's hair and argued about make-up. She wore more than I did; but then a lot of make-up doesn't suit me. It makes me look like a stage barmaid.

When we eventually came down the stairs Dad said 'Hallelujah!' and Mum said tactfully, 'You both look very nice,' but I could see that she was secretly amazed how well my first attempt at dressmaking had turned out. I was pretty amazed myself. The dress made me feel quite different from my usual self. Older, for a start. And really rather slinky.

Rupert said, 'Pity you couldn't have got the hemline straight all the way round. I suppose there wasn't enough bedspread to make a proper dress?'

I refrained from biffing him, because it wouldn't have been dignified, but it took all my self-control.

Dad said, 'Take no notice, Harriet. You look extremely elegant.'

'So do you,' I told him, which was no more than the truth. He always looked good in his dinner jacket.

On the drive to the dance both Julie and I sat in the back seat with Dad in front like a chauffeur. Julie whispered to me, 'I'm a bit nervous. How about you?'

'Not too bad.' I hadn't told her yet about the quiz. It seemed best to wait until after I'd talked to J.J.

'You don't think my dress is dated, do you? I mean, yours looks so modern.'

'It *is* modern. We only finished it yesterday.'

She said glumly, 'I wish we could have made something new for me to wear as well.'

'We didn't have the time. Anyway, don't worry, Hamish will think your red dress is a knockout.'

But I could tell by the way she kept fiddling with the bow and twitching her taffeta skirt that she wasn't any too confident.

Dad drove us right up to the school building so we wouldn't have to walk too far. As we got out of the car two figures detached themselves from the shadows under the archway. The first I recognised as Hamish, although there was something odd about his silhouette: it was too dark to make out what. Behind him hovered a slightly-built boy with hair so fair he looked almost bald in the moonlight.

'There are your escorts,' Dad said. 'I'll leave you

76

in their capable hands while I go and park the car. See you inside.'

'Okay.' I bent to whisper to him through the open car window, 'You won't forget, will you – about asking J.J.?'

He grinned. 'First thing we have to do is track him down. My guess is he won't stay at the dance a moment longer than he has to.' He wound up the window and drove off.

Hamish pulled forward his companion. 'This is Dave.'

'Hi, Dave,' I said. 'I'm Harriet. This is Julie.'

Dave cleared his throat and croaked, 'Hi.'

We all four stood smiling foolishly at each other.

'Let's go inside,' Hamish said.

He showed us where to leave our coats, then led us through the cloisters to Great School, which was what St Olav's called its assembly hall. This was a huge, wood-panelled room with portraits of past headmasters glaring down from the walls – not exactly the perfect venue for a disco, although someone had fixed up some strobe lighting. At the far end, on a dais, a couple of boys were operating the sound equipment, while around the edge were wooden chairs, mostly occupied by anxious-looking girls from the Convent. Groups of boys lurked at a safe distance, casting them surreptitious glances. A few couples were already dancing, somewhat half-heartedly, under the watchful eye of about a dozen members of staff, including three nuns.

'Oh, glory!' Julie muttered under her breath.

I thought she was commenting on the set-up, then realised she was staring at Hamish. Now we were in the lighted room I could see what was different about him. He was wearing full Highland regalia, complete with green velvet jacket and white lace jabot – and he looked sensational.

'Wow!' I exclaimed. 'I've never seen you in a kilt before. What's the tartan?'

'Hunting Stewart,' he said. 'Would you like to dance?'

By this time I'd already scanned the room pretty thoroughly for J.J. and discovered he wasn't there, so I said, 'Okay. Although our skirts may clash if we whirl around too fast. I suppose I'd better not ask the obvious question?'

'Red flannel boxer shorts,' he said, without a glimmer of a smile.

Well, how about that! Hamish McDermid had a dry sense of humour and I'd never realised. I shot him an appreciative grin and we moved on to the floor.

Disco-dancing in a kilt, he could easily have cut a comic figure, but somehow he didn't. Incredibly, he seemed quite unconscious of the fact that everyone in the room was staring at him with open admiration, including the nuns. As we danced, however, I became aware of at least one pair of eyes sending accusing darts in my direction.

Julie's.

Left with no alternative but to jig around with

the blushing, painfully shy Dave Wilcox, she was clearly not enjoying herself. This was not what she'd expected. But it was also embarrassingly clear that Hamish regarded *me* as his partner.

'Hamish,' I said at last, 'would you do me a favour?'

'What's that?'

'Give Julie a break from Dave. I think she needs one.'

He glanced across the floor. 'Dave's a nice guy, when you get to know him.'

'I'm sure he is. But he's nowhere near such a good dancer as you are.' I was trying hard to be diplomatic.

Hamish gave me a puzzled look. 'Okay,' he said. 'If it's what you want.'

We moved towards them. 'Change partners,' I sang out, when we were close enough. Julie looked much as Baden-Powell must have looked at the Relief of Mafeking.

I soon realised why. Poor Dave was very heavy-going, in more ways than one. It was like dancing with a bashful hippopotamus.

Soon afterwards another group of boys appeared, with some of the Sixth Form girls, and I looked again for J.J., but he wasn't among them. Then Dad came in behind them – I guessed he'd just rounded them up, like a sheep-dog, and herded them into Great School – so I excused myself from Dave and went over to him.

'Did you see J.J.?' I asked.

'Not yet. Isn't he here?'

'Not a sign of him.'

'Never mind, he's sure to turn up when it's supper-time. They do a good buffet on these occasions. Even the most dance-shy boys usually come out of their bolt-holes when they smell food.'

'I hope you're right,' I said. 'Because I can't wait to tell him about you-know-what.'

Dad said casually, 'Plenty of time.'

It was all right for him, but I was growing impatient. I felt that if I didn't see J.J. soon and find out what his answer was, I'd burst.

Supper-time arrived and still no sign of J.J. My eyes ached from watching the door.

'More chicken, Harriet?' Hamish was being very attentive.

'No, thanks.'

'Okay, let's grab ourselves some chairs.'

On our way over to a table Julie muttered, 'Harriet, are you okay?'

'Yes, fine.'

'Sure you're not upset about something?'

'No. Why should I be?'

'You seem sort of distracted. I just wondered if you . . . well, minded?'

'Minded about what?'

She lowered her voice still further. 'Hamish and me. Only I think he quite likes me. Are you sure you don't want him for yourself.'

Something inside me seemed to snap. 'How many times do I have to tell you, Julie? *No, I do not want him for myself.* I have other fish to fry.'

She looked hurt. 'What fish?'

'Never you mind.' When we reached the table I

put down my plate and said to Hamish, 'Will you excuse me a moment. I have to go somewhere.'

'Do you know where it is?' he inquired. 'Shall I show you?'

'Not *there*!' I snapped. 'And I can find my way around this place without any help, thanks. My father's been teaching here long enough.' They all stared at me, obviously mystified by my sudden display of bad temper. A little ashamed, I muttered, 'Shan't be long,' and made my exit.

It was true that I knew my way to Burton House, because that's where Dad, being house tutor, had his study. I also knew where the senior boys' rooms were, along the corridor on the ground floor. A few people gave me curious glances, but I assumed a purposeful air and charged on, hoping that if they recognised me they'd assume I was looking for Dad.

It wasn't difficult to find J.J.'s room. His name was on the door. I took a deep breath and knocked twice.

'Enter if you must.'

Not exactly encouraging. I opened the door cautiously.

He was writing at his desk by the harsh light of an anglepoise lamp, which made his thin face look paler than ever. When I entered he looked up at me without recognition.

'Hello, J.J. I'm Harriet Bowles.'

Why, oh why, did I always have to re-introduce myself every time we met? Couldn't he – just once – have looked as if he knew who I was?

'What on earth are you doing here?' he demanded. 'Girls aren't allowed —'

'Yes, I know,' I interrupted. 'But this is important. May I come in?'

'I'd prefer you didn't.'

Too late. I was already inside. I closed the door discreetly behind me and started talking fast. 'Listen, you know the programme Youth Challenge?' When he shook his head I said, 'You must do. It's on television twice weekly, Tuesdays and Thursdays. Kids from all over the country take part.'

'I already told you, I don't watch television.'

I could have shaken him. 'Anyway, Tom Byford – he's the man who organised the trivia quiz at the Town Hall, remember? – wants to enter a team from Bradley and he's chosen us.'

J.J. stared at me blankly.

'You and me.' I spoke extra clearly, determined to get the message over to him. Really, for someone so bright he was remarkably slow on the uptake. 'Because we're the ones who did best. It has to be a boy and a girl, you see, but it doesn't matter if we come from different schools. It's the town we'll be representing.'

J.J. frowned. 'Your father hasn't mentioned it.'

'He will as soon as he sees you. He thought you'd come to the dance.'

'I never go to dances,' he said loftily. 'That kind of primitive tribal custom doesn't appeal to me.'

'Nor me,' I assured him. 'The only reason I'm here is because I wanted to ask you about the quiz. Dad's promised to give Tom Byford our answer tomorrow. That's why I came to look for you.'

'You're not supposed to be here,' he said again. He seemed far more concerned about my presence in his room than about the quiz.

'I had to see you, J.J.' I moved a couple of books on his desk so that I could perch on the edge. 'To find out how you feel about it.'

'About what?'

'The *quiz*! If the BBC are interested in our application we'd have to go to an audition, but that'll be somewhere fairly local. Then, if we're selected, we'll probably have to go up to Manchester or somewhere for the recording.'

'Is there a prize?'

'Well, there's a trophy if we win the whole contest and a sort of shield thing if we're runners-up.'

'No money?'

'I don't think so. But it'll be a chance in a life-time if we're accepted. I mean, we may never get to go on television again in our entire lives. So – how do you feel?'

Before he could answer the door flew open and two boys stood there. I didn't recognise either of them – and I didn't much care for the expression on their faces, which could only be described as evilly triumphant.

'Well, hello!' murmured the taller of the two, who had black untidy eyebrows that met in the middle. 'Here's something new. The Ferret has a girl in his room.'

'She can't be very fussy,' said the other, who was short and fattish. He pushed his face up close to mine. 'Bit short-sighted, dear, are you?'

'With those glasses she should be able to spot a pimple on the moon.' Eyebrows sniggered. 'They're like a couple of satellite dishes!'

I gave them both a withering look. 'Push off,' I said. 'We're talking business.'

'Oh, business, is it? That's a new name for it.'

'You heard what she said,' J.J. muttered. 'Go away.'

'And leave you alone together?' Eyebrows pretended to be shocked. 'My dear Ferret, will you be safe? She looks a bit predatory to me.'

I slid off the desk and drew myself up to my full height. 'You're right, I *am* predatory. In fact I've been known to eat little boys like you for breakfast and spit out the bones. So hop it, wimpo.'

They both gave an appreciative roar, which must have carried the entire length of the corridor, because seconds later a man's voice said, 'What's going on in here?'

Eyebrows smirked. 'Nothing, Sir. Just talking to Dexter, Sir . . . '

The door was pushed open wider. To my embarrassment I recognised Burton's housemaster, Mr Leggatt, who stared at me in astonishment. 'Harriet Bowles, what on earth are you doing here?'

'Hello, Mr Leggatt. I – er, came to the dance . . . '

'I meant here in one of the boy's rooms. Surely you know that isn't allowed?'

84

'Yes, but I had to talk to J.J. about something. It was important —'

'It doesn't matter how important, you're breaking the rules.' He looked grimly uncompromising. 'I think your father may have something to say about that.'

Eight

I was in the doghouse. Dad, though outwardly calm, was clearly livid with me. Julie and Hamish looked confused and uncomfortable. They didn't, of course, know exactly what had happened, and I made no attempt to tell them. Inwardly I was seething with resentment at the injustice of it all. Such a fuss over an innocent little visit to a boy's room – anyone would think I'd done something really shocking, like a strip-tease in the middle of Great School.

On the way home Dad waited until he'd dropped Julie off and then said, 'Honestly, Harriet, I don't understand how you could be so stupid.'

'I had to see J.J.'

'Why? What was the urgency?'

'You know why, Dad. To ask him about the quiz.'

'You should have left it to me. I'd have got round to it eventually. When he didn't show up at the dance —'

'It was suppertime. You said he'd be sure to come at suppertime, but he didn't.'

'Even so, you shouldn't have gone to his room. You know the rules.'

'If you ask me, they're archaic. At Bradley High they treat us like responsible citizens.'

'St Olav's is a boarding school, Harriet. The rules have to be stricter than for a day school, especially now we have girls in the Sixth Form.' Dad sighed heavily. 'And to think it should be my own daughter . . .'

We both fell silent. I began to have a few qualms of conscience about how I may have damaged Dad's reputation – to say nothing of J.J.'s. The most maddening thing was that I still didn't know J.J.'s answer.

Well, it would almost certainly be 'no'. The last thing he'd want to do was appear on television alongside a girl who'd embarrassed him in front of his housemaster and his friends – if you could call that pair of crude layabouts his friends. He'd probably refuse to have anything to do with me ever again.

As we drew into our drive I asked Dad in a small voice, 'Will you tell Mum?'

'Yes, of course.'

I made it even smaller and added a tragic note. 'You could at least spare me that.'

'Why should I?' he said callously. 'You haven't spared me much.'

'Okay,' I said, my voice returning to normal. 'I'll do a deal with you. Let me tell her myself and – and I'll clean your shoes for you tomorrow.' I knew this was the job he hated more than any other.

After a pause he asked, '*All* my shoes?'

'If you want.'

'Done.'

*   *   *

Unexpectedly, the first thing Mum said when I told her was 'Poor Hamish.'

'Why "poor Hamish"?' I demanded. 'What did it have to do with him?'

'Everything, I'd have thought. You went to the dance at his invitation, as his partner.'

'No, I didn't. I mean – yes, it was Hamish who invited me, but I wasn't exactly his partner.'

'He thought you were.'

I was silent, uneasily aware this was true.

Mum went on, 'I hope you apologised to him?'

'No-o,' I admitted. 'There wasn't much opportunity.'

'In that case you'd better do it tomorrow, when he comes to lunch.'

Hamish coming to Sunday lunch was a ritual by now. He was almost one of the family. Even so, the thought of apologising to him made me feel quite nervous.

Luckily he arrived early, while I was alone in the kitchen. Mum was in the living-room, having a glass of sherry with Dad, while Rupert watched an old episode of *The Waltons* with the sound turned down. The roast was in the oven, smelling fantastic.

Hamish looked at the pairs of Dad's shoes I'd lined up on newspaper. They ranged from heavy-duty mud-beaters to his best leather casuals. 'Do you always clean your father's shoes for him?' he asked.

'Not if I can help it,' I said frankly. 'It's a kind of penance for the way I behaved last night. And I'd like to apologise to you too, Hamish, if I embarrassed you in any way. I didn't mean to.'

He looked faintly puzzled, but didn't say anything.

I said, 'You do know what happened, don't you? About me going to J.J.'s room, I mean. I only wanted to find out whether he'd be on the quiz team with me, but then these two boys came along and – oh, I don't know. The whole thing was just too stupid for words.'

Hamish's face cleared. 'Oh, that. Aye, I did hear about it.'

I asked suspiciously, 'Why, what did you think I meant?'

He shrugged.

'Oh, come on – what else did I do that could have embarrassed you?'

'Well,' he began hesitantly, 'to be honest, I think you may have misled your friend Julie. She seemed to have got hold of the wrong idea.'

'About being your partner, you mean? I'm sorry, Hamish, but there was a reason for that. The fact is, she likes you a lot – and she was really really keen to meet you again.'

'I did rather get that impression.' He didn't sound as if it pleased him one bit.

'You should be flattered,' I said. 'Julie's a very popular girl at Bradley High. She has loads of boyfriends.'

'Maybe that's the trouble,' he said drily. 'I don't care for being one of a crowd – just another scalp to add to her belt.'

'Oh, you wouldn't be, I'm sure. Julie's not like that. She really does like you, Hamish.'

'And I like her. But that's as far as it goes – okay?' For a moment he looked quite fierce.

'Yes, okay,' I muttered hastily.

It occurred to me that the reason he and Julie had looked so confused and uncomfortable last evening may have had nothing to do with me at all. One way and another, the occasion had been a total disaster.

I asked tentatively, 'Did J.J. get into trouble?'

'I don't believe so.' Hamish picked up the shoe I'd just put polish on and started to brush it.

'I'd feel awful if he did, because it wasn't his fault.' I added gloomily, 'The worst part is, he'll never agree to be on the quiz team with me now.'

'Oh yes, he will,' Hamish said.

I stared at him. 'How do you know?'

'Because he's said so. He's gone round telling everyone this morning he's going to be on television. He seems quite excited about it.'

'He does?' I could hardly believe what I was hearing. 'In spite of what happened last night?'

'More likely *because* of what happened last night.' A flicker of a grin crossed Hamish's face. 'You did wonders for his reputation, Harriet.'

'I thought I'd ruined it.'

'Are you mad? J.J. Dexter caught with a girl in his room – suddenly everyone's looking at him in an entirely different light. He's always been known as – well, frankly, a bit of a non-starter where girls are concerned. But now, amazingly, he's Don Juan.'

It took me a moment to digest this. 'Hamish,' I said, 'why did those boys – the ones who discovered us last night – call him the Ferret?'

'Because he looks like one,' Hamish said.

There was, I had to admit, some truth in this. J.J.'s nose was long and rather ferret-like; and his eyes were a bit on the small side.

'I expect it's his brains that make him unpopular,' I said, determined to defend him. 'People are always suspicious of somebody who knows a lot. I suffer from much the same problem.' I added hastily, 'Not that I'm in J.J.'s class, of course. He's a true intellectual, whereas I tend to be butterfly-minded. But I know how it feels to be regarded as a bit of an oddball.'

Again there was a suspicion of a grin on Hamish's face.

'Are you absolutely sure,' I asked, 'that he wants to be on Youth Challenge with me?'

'Oh, yes.'

'But that's great!' Suddenly the whole day was transformed. The events of last night seemed unimportant. Nothing mattered except that J.J. and I would be together again – this time on television! Flushed with relief and pleasure and a whole lot of other emotions, I turned to the door. 'I must tell Dad — '

But at that moment the door opened and Mum came in. 'Oh hello, Hamish,' she said. 'I didn't know you'd arrived. Harriet, will you please clear those shoes off the table? I want to make a batter.'

'In a minute,' I said. 'I have to see Dad — '

'No, *now*.'

Reluctantly I started to clear the table. While I was folding up the soiled newspaper she caught my eye and raised her eyebrows questioningly. It took me a moment to twig that she wanted to know if I'd apologised to Hamish. I nodded.

She took a pyrex mixing bowl out of the cupboard. 'It's not long before the end of term. Will you be spending Easter with your father, Hamish, or are you going to your aunt's?'

'I don't know yet,' he said. 'Dad's not too sure of his plans.'

She tied an apron around her waist. 'You'd be very welcome to stay with us, you know, if you don't want to go up to Aberdeen.'

He looked at her uncertainly and then at me. I sensed he was waiting for me to say something, so I murmured, 'Yes, why don't you? It'd be fun.'

He turned to Mum. 'Thanks very much, Mrs Bowles. I'd like that, if I can't go to my father's. Will it be all right if I let you know in a week or so?'

'Any time,' Mum said.

I stowed the shoes in a cardboard box, to be transported upstairs later, and went straight to the living-room.

Dad was reading the newspaper. When I told him the news he said calmly, 'Yes, I know.'

I gaped at him. 'How?'

'J.J. caught me this morning after Chapel. I rang Tom Byford as soon as I got home. He was delighted.'

I said indignantly, 'Well, you might have told me!'

'I didn't think it would do you any harm to stew for a while.' Dad turned the paper inside-out, looking for the crossword puzzle.

Rupert tore his gaze from the TV. 'Does that mean Harriet will definitely be on television?'

'Provided she gets through the audition without making a hash of things, yes,' Dad said.

'She better hadn't,' Rupert said, turning back to the screen.

Next day at school Julie was decidedly cool towards me, so I took her aside at break and said, 'Look, I'm sorry if things didn't work out between you and Hamish on Saturday, but it wasn't my fault. I did my best for you.'

She gave me an odd look. 'Harriet, for someone who's supposed to be smart you can sometimes be incredibly dense.'

'What do you mean?'

'Only that I never stood a chance with Hamish right from the start – because, Harriet Bowles, the only person he's the least bit interested in is *you*.'

I couldn't have been more stunned if she'd hit me over the head with her maths book. 'You're nuts!'

'No, I'm not. I suspected it that day at the rugger match, when I went to find out if he was hurt. But when he saw me the first thing he said was, "Where's Harriet?" It was perfectly obvious that you were the only person he cared about.'

This explained why Julie had appeared to go off

him for a while. I asked, 'So why did you come to the dance?'

'Because you said he wanted me to. But when we got there I realised I'd been right all along. He never took his eyes off you for a minute.'

I shook my head. 'It's impossible.'

'Harriet! Why else do you think he comes over to your house so often?'

'To work on my father's car. And because he likes being with a family – at least, that's what Mum thinks.'

'Then she's as blind as you are.' Julie turned away to join the coffee queue.

'Well, I hope you're wrong,' I muttered, following her. 'I mean, I like Hamish okay, but he's not at all my type.'

'So you keep telling me.' She sounded almost weary. 'You also said you had other fish to fry.'

'So I do.'

'Who, then? Surely not Harvey Feldman?'

'No, of course not!' I looked round furtively, to make sure no one else was plugging into our conversation. 'If I tell you, will you promise to keep it to yourself?' She nodded. 'Okay. Well, it's J.J. Dexter.' As soon as I'd said his name I could feel myself going hotly pink.

'You're joking!'

'No, I'm not.'

'But he's so pompous! You can't honestly tell me you prefer that long-nosed twit to someone like Hamish?'

'I'm different from you,' I said huffily. 'You drool

over boys' legs on the rugger field, but it's J.J.'s intelligence that knocks me out.'

For a moment Julie was silent. Then she said, 'You've got me wrong, you know. It's true that Hamish has fantastic legs – did you get a load of his knees under that kilt? – but he also has a nice character. That's just as important to me as his looks.'

'It wasn't his character you noticed when you saw him from my bedroom window,' I reminded her. 'You just thought he was a gorgeous hunk.'

'So he is. But he's a lot more besides – sensitive, caring . . . ' She added with a hint of reproach, 'I think he could easily be hurt.'

This conversation was making me feel worse every minute. The last thing I wanted was for Hamish to be nurturing an unrequited passion for me when I needed all my energy to cope with my own unrequited passion for J.J. But Julie had to be wrong. She'd misread the signs and come up with a convenient theory as to why she hadn't clicked with Hamish. By the end of that day I'd pretty well managed to convince myself that this was the only logical explanation.

All the same, I looked forward to my next meeting with Hamish in a somewhat nervous frame of mind.

Nine

I hardly saw Hamish during the last two weeks of term, but when I did, I couldn't detect the least sign in his behaviour that he was harbouring this great secret passion for me that Julie was so sure about. He was just his usual calm, not-very-talkative self.

What's more, he didn't jump at Mum's invitation to stay with us during the Easter vacation, but said his father would be in England right up until the last four days, so would it be okay if he came to us for three nights prior to the beginning of term? Mum said that would be fine.

But if he was really keen, I thought, he'd have found some excuse to spend a lot longer than that with us. So I decided to put the whole idea right out of my mind and not let it spoil things.

In any case my mind was already fully occupied with thoughts of the audition, which was to be held at a hotel in Bristol on the day before St Olav's summer term began. This meant that J.J., who lived in Bath, would have to meet us there.

The prospect of seeing him again coloured the entire holiday. Hardly a day went by without me thinking about it and wondering how it would all turn out. Not even a week in Cornwall visiting Dad's parents, or five days in Wales visiting

Mum's, banished it from my mind. As the time came nearer I began to wish I'd never let myself in for such a nerve-wracking ordeal.

On the evening before the audition I couldn't sit still. After supper everyone else flonked out in front of the television, but I was so restless I kept pacing the room. In the end Dad suggested I went for a walk.

'Not on her own,' Mum said quickly. 'It wouldn't be safe.'

In fact Bradley was not a violent town, at least not around where we lived, but Mum always worked on the principle that anywhere can be dangerous after dark.

'Hamish will go with her,' Dad said. 'Won't you, Hamish?'

Hamish had arrived two days ago. Obediently he got to his feet. 'Aye, I'd be glad of the chance to stretch my legs.'

This was embarrassing. So far I'd taken care not to be alone with him, just in case. What Julie had said still troubled me, even though I couldn't believe she was right.

'Oh, don't bother,' I said, practically pushing him back on to the sofa. 'It's raining anyway.'

'No, it's not,' said Rupert. 'It's stopped.'

Hamish stood up again. 'Come on, Harriet. It'll do us both good.'

There was no getting out of it. 'Okay,' I said resignedly.

It wasn't completely dark outside, because the sun had only just gone down and the sky was still light around the edges. Nor was it raining, although the air felt damp and chilly. 'Where d'you want to go?' I asked ungraciously.

Hamish closed the gate behind us. 'I don't mind. You know this part of town better than I do. You choose.'

Actually there wasn't much choice. We could go either down by the canal or across the recreation ground. I tossed a mental coin and opted for the canal.

As we walked along the tow-path I asked him where his father had gone this time and he said, 'Mexico.'

'Gosh, that sounds glamorous. Couldn't you have gone with him?'

He shook his head. 'I'd be in the way.'

'Why, what does he do?'

'Makes film documentaries for television. He's a freelance producer.'

I stopped dead. 'Your father works in television? Why didn't you tell us?'

'You never asked me.'

It sounded like a reproach, but I refused to feel guilty. The main reason I hadn't asked Hamish about his father was because I didn't want to pry into his family affairs, which was obviously a sensitive area. 'So what kind of programmes does he make?'

'Mainly archaeological – you know, ancient historical sites. They showed one of his a couple of months ago, about Crete.'

'I think I saw it. There was a man in shorts

sitting on a fallen pillar and talking a lot. Was that your father?'

'No, he never appears in front of camera – or anywhere else if he can help it. They asked him once to come and give a talk at St Olav's, but he refused. He hates speaking in public.'

He sounded a bit like Hamish. 'Do you take after him?' I asked.

'In some ways. Except I don't have his brains, unfortunately. And I conform much more than he does. He likes living rough in solitary places. I'm happier being one of the crowd.'

We were coming to a bridge over the canal. Underneath it was black as pitch and our voices echoed against the brickwork. I said, 'You think a lot of him, don't you?'

'He's the most interesting man in the world.'

Maybe it was the echo that made Hamish sound so dramatic. His words were still ringing in my ears when we came out the other side of the bridge. I asked, 'Is that why you chose to live with him rather than your mother?'

For a moment there was silence and I wondered if I'd put my foot in it. Then he said slowly, 'I didn't exactly choose, you know. When my parents broke up I went out to Canada with the rest of the family, but I only stayed six months.'

'Didn't you like it there?'

'Canada was okay. It was me that was wrong. I couldn't get on with my stepfather.'

This surprised me. Hamish seemed so easy-going I'd have thought he could get on with anybody. 'Was he difficult?'

100

'Not particularly. But I was older than the other two. At thirteen I found it hard to accept that my mother had stopped loving my father and married someone else. I resented him and I'm afraid it showed.'

I tried to put myself in his place. If Mum left Dad and went off with another man . . . But I couldn't even bear to think of it. 'I'd have been the same,' I said.

'Anyway, things obviously weren't working out, mainly because I kept going on about Dad and what a marvellous person he was. In the end Mum said, "Why don't you go and live with him, then, if he's so marvellous?" I don't blame her for losing patience with me. I must have been driving her mad.'

'And that's what you did?'

'Not straight away. There were endless rows and long telephone discussions; but in the end – yes, Dad agreed to take me back, provided I didn't mind going to boarding school. Obviously he couldn't have me with him all the time because of his job.' Hamish kicked a stray stone off the path and it fell with a plop into the inky waters of the canal. 'It wasn't the perfect solution, but it was the best possible in the circumstances.'

I sensed a certain tension in his manner and wondered if I'd done the right thing in getting him to talk about it. In a sudden need to show my sympathy I slipped my arm through his. 'You're not sorry that you came back to live in England?'

'No, it's made me grow up. I can't be dependent on my father, because I know now that he's basically a loner, so I've learned to depend on myself. When I think back to that spoilt kid who caused all those rows in Canada I can't believe it was me.'

'But you don't want to go back?'

'Not for good. It's okay going for a short visit, but that's enough.'

It was dark now, so we left the tow-path and walked home through the wet streets, still arm-in-arm. I was glad Hamish had told me about his parents and no longer felt any awkwardness about being with him. It was as if his telling me had changed things between us in some way.

It had also taken my mind right off tomorrow.

The audition was fixed for 2.30 p.m. It was Dad's idea that the whole family, including Hamish, should come with us in the car to Bristol. We'd meet J.J. off the train and all go to lunch together; then, when J.J. and I went off to the hotel, the others would go shopping. In theory it sounded fine.

The reality was that J.J. missed his train and was forty-five minutes late arriving, which meant we lost the table Dad had booked at the restaurant and had to wait until another one was free. I didn't mind too much because I wasn't hungry, but I felt embarrassed because J.J. hadn't apologised and I could tell that Mum, who'd never met him before, wasn't impressed.

When we eventually sat down to eat Dad said, 'Right, now what's everybody going to have?'

J.J. scanned the menu with a frown. Even after

the rest of us had given our order he still hadn't made up his mind. I saw that Dad was getting impatient and said, 'I expect J.J. doesn't have much appetite, like me. You can't blame us for being nervous about the audition.'

J.J. looked at me in astonishment. 'I'm not nervous. Why should I be nervous?' He closed the menu. 'I'll have a steak, please. Medium rare. No chips.'

'No chips?' Rupert said incredulously.

'I don't care for too much carbohydrate. It doesn't suit my metabolism.'

This remark was greeted by silence. In my brightest voice, about two tones higher than usual, I said, 'Did you have a good holiday, J.J.?'

'Yes, excellent. We went to Italy.'

'Italy? How lovely,' Mum said. 'Which part?'

'Milan. My father took me there specially to see a new chemical plant that's just been built. It's one of the most revolutionary in Europe.'

At that point I intercepted a look between Mum and Dad and realised they were secretly laughing at J.J. This made me so furious that I leaned across the table to say, 'Let's hope the TV people ask you some science questions, J.J. If they do we'll get through easily.'

He gave a slight shrug, as if it had never occurred to him we could do anything else.

Rupert said, with a dreamy expression, 'I expect you'll meet Sue Morrison.'

'Not today,' I said. 'She's hardly likely to turn up at the audition. I don't suppose we'll meet her till the actual programme.'

'Who's Sue Morrison?' J.J. inquired.

'She's the person who asks the questions.' Rupert stared at him. 'Don't you ever watch Youth Challenge?'

'He doesn't watch television at all,' I explained. 'He thinks it's a waste of time.'

There was another strained silence. Making conversation with J.J. around could be heavy-going, I thought. But of course someone with his towering intellect wouldn't find it easy to make small talk. Anyway, Hamish wasn't much better. J.J.'s presence seemed to inhibit him in some way.

I was relieved when lunch was over and we were on our way to the hotel. At the foot of the steps the rest of the family said goodbye and wished us good luck. Then it was just J.J. and me, on our own – apart from about thirty other kids who were there for the same purpose. At the sight of them my spirits sank. They all looked so darned *bright*.

The first thing we had to do was complete a general knowledge paper, twenty questions, not too difficult, in ten minutes. Then we were told to wait in a sort of ante-room for the interview. J.J. and I took our places on a couple of high-back chairs.

'If it's alphabetical,' I muttered, 'we should get in quite early. I'm Bowles, you're Dexter and we come from Bradley.'

But as the minutes ticked by it became clear that whatever system they were using, it certainly wasn't alphabetical. J.J. took a paperback book from his pocket and started to read. I stole a crafty look at the title. It was called *A Study of Molecular Structure*.

'I hate this waiting,' said the girl sitting next to me. 'It gets on my nerves.'

'Mine too,' I agreed.

'The trouble is, you have to *appear* confident, otherwise you don't stand a chance. It's not just brains they're looking for, it's a sparky personality.'

'I suppose it is.' I cast a doubtful look at J.J., still deep in his book. By no stretch of the imagination could you say that he had a sparky personality. I wasn't even sure that I had; but at least I looked pretty colourful in my red ski pants and the stripey shawl-type top I'd made during the holidays. Inspired by the success of my dress for the dance, I'd been quite bitten lately by the dressmaking bug.

There were just six of us left when suddenly Hamish came in. I'd never been so pleased to see anyone in my life. J.J. looked up and grunted when he joined us, then went back to his book.

'I got bored with shopping,' Hamish said, 'so I thought I'd come and see how things were going?'

'They aren't,' I said. 'We haven't been called yet.'

He took the now-empty chair beside me. 'Would you like me to wait with you?'

'Yes, please. I'd be glad of the company.'

It didn't occur to me till after I'd said it that this was an odd remark, considering J.J. was present.

At last a woman appeared from the inner sanctum and said, 'Harriet Bowles and Jeremy Dexter, please.'

I nudged J.J. and he put his book away. As we got to our feet Hamish gave us the thumbs-up sign. I smiled feebly, but all I could think as we walked across the room was that J.J. didn't look in the least like a Jeremy. It made him sound like a different person.

'Hi, come in.' A tall girl with severely short hair stood up to shake hands with us. 'I'm Sandra Wymark, one of the researchers on the programme. And this is Perry Williams, the assistant producer.'

Perry Williams, who was short and balding, waved a hand at us without getting up. I reckoned he must already have seen so many would-be contestants that he was feeling punch-drunk.

Sandra Wymark did most of the talking. She started by asking us some fairly routine questions about Bradley as a town and our respective schools. To my relief, J.J. was now looking very alert, leaning forward in his seat and giving her some full and – I thought – impressive answers. When she asked him what were his ambitions, he told her about going to university and said he hoped to enter industry as a research chemist. She wrote everything down, then turned to me.

'Now Harriet, how about you?'

'My ambitions? Er . . . ' Stupidly, I'd been so busy listening to J.J.'s answers I hadn't thought out what I was going to say. 'Well, I'm not too sure at the moment. I mean, I'm not good at anything much except Trivial Pursuit.'

She said drily, 'It might be hard to make a career out of Trivial Pursuit.'

Oh heck, I'd blown it! Why on earth hadn't I foreseen they'd ask these sort of questions? In a last ditch attempt to save the situation I burbled, 'Actually, what I'd really like to do is become the world's first four-eyed fashion model. I mean, you don't often see girls in glasses gliding down the catwalk, do you, so I reckon it's about time somebody acknowledged our existence. In fact I'm thinking of starting up a new movement – Owls' Lib.'

Sandra Wymark's gaze flickered over my spectacles and down to my stripey top. 'Well, you obviously have an eye for the unusual.'

I said modestly, 'Oh, this is just something I made myself, out of an old table-cloth my mother threw out. It was only my second attempt at dressmaking, and this time I didn't use a pattern, so I'm quite pleased with the way it's turned out. My friend Julie likes it so much she's asked me to make her one as well, except she's buying the material specially because she doesn't have any tablecloths at home. They use dinner-mats . . .' My voice trailed off as I caught sight of the expression on J.J.'s face. He was looking at me as if I'd gone stark, staring mad.

I glanced quickly at Perry Williams. He looked a bit stunned as well.

'Sorry,' I muttered. 'You're not interested in all this.'

'We're interested in everything,' Sandra Wymark said smoothly. 'Now let me explain the procedure if you're accepted.'

Briefly, the programme would be recorded in

107

Manchester and they hoped to get through four shows a day. If we had to stay overnight accommodation would be provided at a nearby hotel. But of course how long we stayed would depend on whether or not we got through the first round.

'Anyway, thanks for coming.' She showed us to the door. 'We'll let you know within a couple of weeks if you've been successful.'

Once outside, I muttered under my breath, 'Don't ring us, we'll ring you.'

Hamish stood up as soon as he saw us. 'How did it go?'

'Ask Harriet.' J.J. stalked grimly past him. 'She's the one who's just wrecked our chances.'

Ten

For the next two weeks I wallowed in a positive orgy of self-hate. How could I have said such idiotic things, especially when I hadn't the least desire to become a fashion model? Just about the last thing I wanted was to spend my life climbing in and out of clothes and cavorting around to music on a catwalk. In my panic I'd said the first thing that came into my head. Now J.J. would never want to have anything to do with me ever again.

When I related the whole dismal tale to Julie she said, 'That just proves he's not worth bothering about. He can't have an ounce of humour or he'd have seen the funny side.'

'There wasn't a funny side,' I said mournfully.

'Oh Harriet, snap out of it! It's probably all for the best. You've plenty to think about this term, what with exams and things, without having to worry about any old quiz.'

She was right, of course. I could see that. But it wasn't just any old quiz, it was Youth Challenge, and I regretted bitterly messing up our chances of representing Bradley on television. What's more, I knew that Dad was disappointed, although he tried not to show it, and so was Rupert. Only Mum seemed a little relieved.

Then one Saturday Tom Byford called round, waving a white envelope. 'It's from the BBC,' he said. 'Great news – we've been selected!'

At first I thought he was joking, but it turned out he wasn't. Even so, I had to read the letter about six times before I believed it. It was impersonally worded, obviously intended for all successful candidates, and gave information about the time and place of the recording, as well as advice on what to wear. But at the bottom there was a handwritten note saying, 'Please ask Harriet Bowles to wear the same clothes as for the audition. S.W.'

S.W. was presumably Sandra Wymark. 'But what do they mean?' I asked, puzzled. '"The same clothes" . . . I don't understand.'

'Well, you did look rather eyecatching that day,' Dad said. 'I expect they want a repeat performance.'

I shook my head. 'That's impossible. You didn't hear how stupid I was.'

'They probably think you'll make a good comic turn,' Rupert said. 'They have people like that sometimes, to get a few laughs.'

'Gee, thanks!' I said, with heavy sarcasm.

'Take no notice, Harriet,' said Tom Byford. 'You'll do Bradley proud, I'm sure.'

After he had gone Dad went up to St Olav's to tell J.J. the good news. I wished like anything I could be a fly on the wall. I'd have loved to see J.J.'s face when he learned I hadn't ruined everything after all.

Later that day Hamish arrived to check the cooling system on Dad's car, which had been overheating lately. While he was fiddling around under the bonnet I asked him if he'd heard about the quiz and he said yes, J.J. had gone round telling everybody. 'Congratulations, Harriet,' he added. 'I knew you couldn't have done as badly as you thought.'

'Oh yes, I did,' I said. 'It must have been J.J.'s brains that got us through. Is he pleased about it?'

'Well, he's trying to be very cool and laid-back about the whole thing, but – yes, I think secretly he's chuffed to bits.'

'Oh, good,' I said, hoping that next time we met he'd look at me quite differently, and not as though I'd just crawled out from under a cow-pat. We were partners now, for better or for worse. I went on casually, 'It might be a good idea if he and I met up some time to discuss tactics. What do you think?'

There was a pause while Hamish continued fiddling. Then he said, 'It depends what you have in mind. Did you want to come up to St Olav's?'

'Er, no,' I said hastily. 'I don't think that would be a very good idea, not after last time.'

'Then why don't you get your father to invite him here, for Sunday lunch?'

That didn't seem a good idea either. I'd spend the entire mealtime worrying in case J.J. said something to make Mum and Dad exchange amused looks again.

'We could meet in town,' I said. 'Could you suggest the Diamond Café?'

The Diamond Café was a favourite place for the High School kids to congregate, mainly because the tables were in little booths, which made it easier to carry on a private conversation. Sometimes St Olav boys came in as well, so it wouldn't be all that unusual for J.J. and me to meet there.

'You want me to ask him?' Hamish didn't sound too keen.

'If you wouldn't mind.'

'Okay, I'll see what I can do.'

'Thanks, Hamish.' I gave him a brilliant smile, which was entirely lost because he was still bent over the engine. 'Tell him three o'clock next Saturday afternoon.'

Hamish groaned. 'Oh, this is hopeless!'

'What is?'

'Your father's car. It's time he got a new one.'

'He doesn't like new cars,' I said. 'He prefers old ones.'

'There are old cars and old cars. This isn't an antique, it's a heap. The sooner he gets rid of it the better.'

'But he's fond of it. He says it's reliable.'

'Not any more it isn't. It's reached the stage in its life where everything's wearing out at once. Frankly, I don't think I can keep it going much longer.'

I wondered if what Hamish really meant was that he was sick of working on Dad's car. Or, put another way, he'd got bored with spending so much time at our house. For some reason this annoyed me, even in the middle of my being so pleased about the quiz.

I said, 'Well, I don't think you'll ever persuade him to buy a new one. He's too mean.'

Hamish slammed down the bonnet lid. 'I'll have a word with your mother. If anyone can persuade him, she will.'

As he strode off towards the house I called after him, 'You won't forget, will you? About J.J. . . . .'

His reply was inaudible, but I felt confident he wouldn't let me down. Not good old dependable Hamish.

But on the following Saturday, sitting alone in a booth at the Diamond Café, I felt far from confident. I'd tried to persuade Julie to come with me, for moral support, but she'd said, 'No, this time you're on your own. I'm not making up any more foursomes.'

I'd assured her it wouldn't be a foursome, and that she needn't even sit with me if she didn't want to, but she wouldn't budge. So there I sat in a crowded café, spooning sugar into my coffee and staring through the steamed-up window, without any real hope that J.J. would come.

I was almost on the point of giving up when I saw him being practically frog-marched down the road by Hamish. He looked as miserable as sin, his shoulders hunched and his coat collar turned up. They entered the café and came over to my table. 'Well, hello!' I said, trying to sound as if we'd bumped into each other quite by chance.

J.J. gave me a sickly look and said nothing.

'Sit down,' Hamish commanded him. 'I'll get the coffee.'

J.J. slid reluctantly into the seat opposite me. 'I

bet you were surprised,' I said, 'when you heard we'd been selected?'

He shrugged.

'The reason I suggested we met,' I hurried on, 'is because you've never seen the programme, and the format's a bit different from the trivia quiz. The categories aren't the same, for a start. There's Science all right, and Literature, but if they get chosen during the first round we have to be prepared to go on to something else. How are you on Current Affairs?'

'Quite good, I should imagine,' J.J. said nonchalantly. 'I read the *Guardian* every day and listen to "Today in Parliament".'

'In that case you'd better make it your second string. I shall go for Popular Music.'

J.J. looked at me down his long nose and sniffed.

'They also have History and Geography,' I said. 'As well as Sport and Natural History, so there's quite a choice. And then there are two quick-fire general knowledge rounds, like the trivia quiz.'

J.J. looked even sniffier and I remembered that he hadn't been too quick on the buzzer at the Town Hall.

'You are pleased about it, aren't you?' I asked, suddenly worried in case he should back out at the last minute. 'Hamish said you were.'

J.J. managed a tight little smile. 'It'll certainly be a novel experience.'

At this point Hamish appeared with two coffees. He put one down in front of J.J. and took the other off to a nearby table.

'Where's he gone?' J.J. asked, looking round.

'I expect he thinks we want to be left alone,' I said; then, seeing the near-panic in J.J.'s eyes, added quickly, 'So we can discuss our tactics in private.'

'Why, what's private about them?'

'Nothing. But they wouldn't interest Hamish.' Desperate to change the subject I asked, 'Have you decided what clothes you're going to wear?'

'Clothes?' He sounded puzzled. 'I'd assumed we'd be wearing school uniform?'

'Lord, no! They'll want us to look as casual as possible.' I cast a dubious look at the way his shirt collar stuck up over his badly tied St Olav's tie. 'A decent sweater might be safest. Of course it's only the top half that shows on television. It doesn't matter what you wear below the waist.'

'How about you?' His eyes narrowed. 'I trust you'll be wearing something a little more appropriate than you did for the audition?'

'As a matter of fact,' I said, careful to keep any expression out of my voice, 'they've particularly asked me to wear the same outfit. It seems they liked it.'

'Good grief!'

His voice said it all. I stared at him hopelessly, thinking that Julie was right – we had absolutely nothing in common. There was no magic, no instant rapport between us. I was such an abject failure with the opposite sex that I couldn't even click with J.J. Dexter.

'Is that all?' he inquired.

'What?'

'Is that all you wanted to talk to me about?'

'Oh . . . yes.' It seemed best to admit defeat. 'Yes, that's all.'

'In that case I may as well go.' He got to his feet. 'There's a meeting of the Debating Society tonight and I have to prepare my speech.' He edged out of the booth and went without saying goodbye either to me or to Hamish.

He hadn't even drunk his coffee.

Hamish came over to join me, carrying his cup. 'Okay?'

Plunged in gloom, I could only nod my head.

He sat down opposite me. 'You've got a bit of a thing about J.J., haven't you?' he asked gently.

I saw no point in denying it. 'I'm afraid I have.'

'I couldn't believe it at first. I thought it was just because of the quiz you kept wanting to see him. But you really do like him, don't you?'

Miserably I said, 'No, that's what's so strange about it. He's not a very likeable person, is he? But feelings are so mysterious. You don't need to like someone in order to have a thing about them.'

Hamish frowned. 'I'd have thought liking was pretty important.'

'Oh, it is if you're being rational. But what I feel for J.J. isn't really rational at all.' I tried hard to find a way of explaining it. 'I think perhaps it's just the *idea* of J.J. that I like.'

Hamish looked totally perplexed.

I went on, 'You see, boys don't fall for me, on the whole. They think I'm too smart. Actually, I'm not all that smart, but somehow I've acquired that reputation. I think it's partly the glasses. So when I heard about J.J. it occurred to me that he was

116

probably in the same boat. That's why I wanted to meet him.'

'You mean you fell for him before you even met him?'

'Well . . . yes, I suppose in a way I did.'

Hamish gave a low, incredulous whistle. 'You're right, that isn't rational.'

'Anyway, it hasn't worked.' I drained my coffee cup and made an effort to sound lighter-hearted. 'In fact it's pretty obvious he can't even stand the sight of me. So much for my theory that two eggheads would get along well together!'

'That's a duff theory anyhow,' Hamish said. 'You'd have ended up competing with each other, which is fatal. Haven't you ever heard of the attraction of opposites?' Without waiting for my reply he finished his own coffee and stood up. 'Come on, I'll see you home.'

My meeting with J.J. killed much of my enthusiasm for being a contestant on Youth Challenge; but in some ways that may not have been such a bad thing. At least it meant I wasn't counting the days until the recording. On the contrary, time seemed to gallop by so fast that soon we were making definite travel plans about how we were going to get to Manchester.

Tom Byford had arranged for a party of Bradley supporters to be taken by coach on the day of the recording, but the contestants had to arrive the night before, to be ready for a studio rehearsal early next morning. Our hotel bookings were already made and a map supplied showing us how

117

to get there from the station. It was assumed we'd be travelling by train.

But Dad had a different idea. He said it was too much of a cross-country journey by rail from Bradley to Manchester, so he'd drive J.J. and me up there instead.

'Are you mad?' Mum demanded. 'You know the car's not reliable. Hamish says it's trouble on wheels.'

'It's just passed its M.O.T.,' Dad pointed out imperturbably.

'Only thanks to Hamish. What if it breaks down miles from nowhere? Harriet will never forgive you if she misses that quiz.'

'I think Mum's right, Dad,' I said. 'It might be best if we went by train.'

'Nonsense. It's not nearly so convenient. However,' he went on quickly, as Mum and I both got ready to launch further objections, 'if it'll make you both happier, I'll ask Hamish to come with us. Then we'll have our own built-in mechanic if anything should go wrong.'

Mum looked a little happier at this. I was quite pleased about it too, because my feelings for J.J. were still very mixed up and I didn't fancy trying to make polite conversation with him on the journey. Having Hamish along might make things much easier.

'Okay,' I said.

'I only hope you don't live to regret it,' Mum said pessimistically.

Her pessimism proved to be justified. The car broke down just outside Macclesfield – some kind of blockage in the carburettor – and it took Hamish an hour and a half to get it going again. J.J. remained on the back seat, reading the book he had brought with him to allay boredom, while Dad and I wandered around the lay-by, trying to contain our impatience. By the time we got back on the road it was already growing dark.

About an hour later, six miles from Manchester, we hit a patch of oil on the road. The car skidded out of control on to the grass verge and plunged down a bank, coming to rest with a sickening bang against the trunk of a birch tree.

In the unearthly silence that followed all I could hear were muffled groans. And all I could see was the outline of Dad's body slumped over the wheel.

Eleven

'Harriet, you okay?' It was Hamish who spoke, from the back seat.

'Yes . . . I think so.' My voice came out in a kind of croak. 'I'm not sure about Dad . . .'

'Hold on, I'm getting out.'

There was movement in the back of the car. Somebody groaned again, but it must have been J.J. because it didn't come from Dad. He was still silent beside me. I unfastened my safety belt and reached over to try and lift him off the wheel, but he was too heavy. I lifted his face instead and felt a sticky wetness on my fingers.

The passenger door was pulled open and Hamish spoke close to my ear. 'Is he hurt?'

'He's unconscious. And his head's bleeding.'

'There's a torch in the glove compartment. See if you can get it out.'

I tried, but the fastening seemed to be jammed. 'I – can't —'

He leaned across me and wrenched it open by force. As soon as he had the torch in his hand he switched it on and shone it over Dad's face. It showed a thick, dark trickle running down from his hair into his beard.

'Hamish, he looks awful!'

'Okay, don't worry . . .'

His voice was so calm. But I was starting to shake all over and I felt sick with fear. What if Dad was dead? I couldn't hear him breathing . . . And now Hamish had disappeared!

'Hamish,' I called; and when there was no answer I screamed, *'Hamish where are you?'*

'It's all right, I'm here.' His face appeared on the other side of the car, beyond Dad. 'The door's already open. It's only his safety belt that's holding him in place. Harriet, can you get out?'

'I'll try . . . '

My legs felt as though they didn't belong to me. But at least they moved when I asked them to. They weren't broken, or even bleeding as far as I could tell.

As I started to ease myself out of the seat there came another groan from the back. 'What about J.J.?' I asked. 'He sounds in terrible pain . . . '

'I'll see to him in a minute. Come round here as quick as you can.'

The urgency in his voice spurred me into action. I climbed out of the door, which wasn't easy because we were tilted sideways on the slope. In the darkness I could only just make out the shape of the car and the tree we'd crashed into. Dad's side had taken the full force of the impact. The sight of all that bent and buckled metal made me feel even sicker.

I stumbled down the bank to where Hamish was crouching beside Dad. 'Is he still alive?' I asked fearfully.

'Yes, he's alive. He's out cold, though. And his

feet seem to be trapped. That's why I can't get him clear of the car.'

'It won't catch fire, will it?'

'No chance.'

But I had the feeling he only said this to stop me panicking.

Suddenly one of the back doors flew open and J.J. practically fell out, groaning and clutching his stomach. He crawled a few yards across the grass to vomit into a bush.

Hamish shone the torch in his direction. 'You okay?'

J.J. raised his face, blinking in the light. 'No, I'm dying.' But his voice contradicted his words. It sounded strong and slightly pettish.

Hamish turned back to me. 'We need help,' he said. 'Did you notice if we passed any houses in the last couple of miles?'

'No, I was half asleep. But if I get back up to the road I should be able to stop a car.'

'Okay. Here, take the torch.' As I started to stagger up the bank he called after me, 'Harriet — take care.'

Stopping a car proved less easy than it sounded. As soon as I saw headlights coming towards me I waved the torch around in agitated circles, but the first car drove straight past. So did the second, third and fourth. They must have thought I was trying to hijack them. Then, just as I was contemplating doing something really desperate, like standing in the middle of the road and refusing to budge, an articulated truck drew to a halt beside me.

'Where d'you want to go, love?'

'I'm not hitching.' I shone the torch up at the driver's face. He looked craggy and reliable. 'We've had an accident. My father's hurt. I've got to get an ambulance.'

He looked up and down the road. 'So where's the car?'

'Down that bank. We hit a tree.'

For a moment he seemed to be weighing up the chances of my being a hoaxer. Then he said, 'Okay, leave this to me,' and began making a call on his CB radio.

At which point I burst into tears.

It was the sheer relief, I think, of knowing that help was on the way. Later, when we were sitting in the hospital casualty unit, drinking hot, sweet tea, the nurse said I'd been good to stay calm for so long, but I said it was only Hamish who'd kept me calm. If it hadn't been for him I'd have given way to panic long before I did.

Dad had recovered consciousness in the ambulance. He had cuts and abrasions on both legs and one of them was broken. Hamish had cracked a rib and I had a terrible ache in my neck and shoulders, due to the whiplash. J.J. was completely unhurt, apart from a few bruises. The police said we'd all had a very lucky escape.

When they wheeled Dad back from the X-ray unit the first thing he said was, 'Harriet, you didn't ring your mother, did you?'

'No,' I said. 'I was waiting to see — '

'Then don't. There's no need to worry her till the morning. We're all okay and there's nothing she can do from this distance. Where's Hamish?'

'I'm here, sir.'

Dad grabbed his arm. 'Listen, you're in charge from now on. Here's my wallet. Take a taxi to the hotel and make sure Harriet and J.J. get some sleep. They're going to need it before tomorrow.' When I started to protest he said, 'Shut up, Harriet, and do as you're told for once. I want you to take part in that quiz, d'you understand? That's what we came for, so no feeble excuses about not feeling like it. The doctor tells me you're both perfectly okay. J.J.?'

'Here, sir.'

'Don't let her try to back out, right?'

'Right, sir.' J.J.'s face was almost as pale as Dad's. He looked miserable and lost.

Dad squeezed my hand. 'Good luck, both of you. Don't worry about me. I'm fine.'

He didn't look it. His eyes were closing already, as if the effort of telling us all what to do had taken his last reserve of strength. The hospital porter wheeled him away, out of our sight.

Hamish took my arm. 'Come on, Harriet. You heard what he said. We'd better ring for a taxi.'

'I hate leaving him . . . '

'Yes, I know. But he's right, you need some sleep.'

'I'll never sleep, not after what's happened . . . '

'Yes, you will. The doctor's given me some sedatives, for all of us.'

Reluctantly I followed him down the corridor.

At the reception desk he reclaimed our luggage, which the police had brought from the car, and made two 'phone calls. The first was to a taxi rank and the second to the hotel, explaining what had happened and making sure they'd let us in. It was now two a.m.

We waited for the taxi in silence. J.J. still looked lost, as if this was something so completely outside his experience that he didn't know how to deal with it. Shock, I suppose. He seemed quite happy to let Hamish take command and did exactly as he was told, without a murmur. Strangely enough, I came nearer to liking him as a person than I ever had before.

When we arrived at the hotel Hamish signed us in, while J.J. and I stood by like a couple of zombies. The night porter was very sympathetic. He offered to make us a cup of tea, but we said no thanks, we'd already drunk enough tea to last us a lifetime and would rather go straight to bed.

The sedative took a long time to work. The warmth of the bed seemed to bring out the ache in my neck, and every time I started to fall asleep my mind went into an action replay of the crash. If I lived to be a hundred I'd never forget that sickening metallic bang as the car hit the tree. In a way I think I was fighting the sedative, afraid to let myself sleep in case I had nightmares. I hardly gave tomorrow's events a thought. They'd become unimportant after what had happened to us today. No, not today – yesterday. It was already tomorrow . . .

Suddenly there was a knock on my door. Hamish's voice said, 'Harriet? Harriet, are you awake?'

I sat up with a start. Light was streaming into the room through a crack in the curtains. I grabbed my glasses from the bedside locker and looked at my watch. Eight-thirty a.m.

'Harriet!'

'All right, I'm coming!' I pulled on my dressing-gown. As I staggered over to the door I realised how stiff I was. Everything ached, not only my neck and shoulders.

I opened the door. Hamish looked tired, but he was fully dressed. 'Is it Dad?' I asked, clutching at my throat. 'He's not worse . . . '

'No, it's the television people. They're down-stairs, waiting. Everyone's having breakfast.'

I groaned. 'Okay, I'll be as quick as I can.'

'Sure you're all right?'

'More or less. Except that I ache all over. How about you? Does your rib hurt?'

He gave me a fleeting grin. 'Only when I breathe. See you downstairs.'

I closed the door behind him and started to dress.

Twenty minutes later, wearing my stripey top and red ski pants, I entered the hotel dining-room. There was a terrific buzz in the atmosphere, with about twenty other kids sitting around, talking and laughing, obviously keyed up to a high pitch of anticipation. In the normal way of things I'd have revelled in it. As it was I felt curiously detached from it all.

'Here she is!' Sandra Wymark spotted me and

came over at once. 'Harriet, how are you feeling? Your friend Hamish told us what happened. It must have been terrible for you. Did you get any sleep at all?'

'A little.' I looked round for Hamish, but couldn't see him anywhere. J.J. was there, though, tucking into bacon and eggs and talking so earnestly to a couple of other boys that he hadn't even noticed my arrival. He seemed completely recovered.

'If you don't feel like taking part today you must say so,' Sandra went on. 'We always have a couple of standby contestants, so if you'd rather postpone — '

'No, thanks,' I said quickly. The last thing I wanted to do was postpone anything. I just wanted to get it over with as soon as possible. 'I'll be fine, honestly.'

'Well, your partner certainly doesn't look any worse for his experience.' She cast a glance at J.J., who was still absorbed in what looked like some deep philosophical discussion. 'Okay, let me introduce you to Edward. He'll be looking after you today, so if you have any problems just let him know.'

I shook hands with Edward, who was youngish and trendily dressed in baggy cords and a Challenger T-shirt. 'Come and have some breakfast,' he said.

'No, I don't think I — '

'Oh, but you must. It's one of our rules that everyone must eat something before going into the studio, otherwise your gurgling stomach will upset our sound engineers.' He led me over to a table where there was an empty chair. 'This is Harriet, everyone. The reason she wasn't around last night was that she was in a car crash on the way here. Nothing too serious, thank goodness, but treat her gently.'

I was immediately the centre of sympathetic attention. Someone poured me a coffee and somebody else called a waiter to take my order. I told him cereal and toast, please, although I didn't think I'd be able to eat either.

Then I saw Hamish, hovering by the door. I waved to him and he came over at once. 'I just called the hospital.' He pulled up a chair from another table and sat down beside me. 'Your father's doing fine but they want to keep him in a while longer in case of concussion. He sent you his love and said you're not to worry about him, just concentrate on the programme.'

I started to get up. 'I must ring Mum — '

'I already did.' He looked apologetic. 'I thought I'd better let her know before she came, otherwise the shock might be too great. But the coach was leaving Bradley at eight-thirty, so it was no use waiting for you to wake up.'

My throat felt dry. 'How did she take it?'

'Pretty well. As soon as they arrive at the studios she'll leave Rupert with me and take a taxi to the hospital to see your father. With luck she may be back in time to see you perform, but if not she says she knows you'll understand.'

I could feel tears pricking behind my eyes and hastily forced a smile. 'Did she say "I told you so"?

Because she could, couldn't she, after warning us not to take the car?'

Hamish shook his head. 'I think she was too relieved we were all alive.'

'But if you hadn't come with us . . . ' A lump stuck in my throat. 'Hamish, I'll never be able to thank you — '

'It's okay,' he interrupted with a smile. 'You don't need to say anything. Just eat your breakfast.'

The waiter had arrived with my order. Obediently I turned around and made a real effort to look as if I wanted to eat, aware that both Hamish and Edward were keeping a watchful eye on me. It wasn't easy, but I had to admit that I felt better afterwards. When I was drinking my coffee Hamish said, 'Harriet, I'm going upstairs to pack. If you need me, my room number's 309.'

'Okay,' I said. 'See you.'

As he walked away the girl sitting next to me, who'd told me her name was Roseanne, gave me a nudge. 'Is he your partner?'

'No, that's my partner, over there.' I pointed out J.J., who now seemed involved in a fairly heated argument. 'Hamish only came along – well, to give us moral support, really.' I didn't want to mention the car: I hated even thinking about it.

'Oh, so he's your boyfriend.' Roseanne gazed admiringly after Hamish's retreating backview. 'He's quite a hunk.'

It was beginning to annoy me, the way the entire female population of this country seemed to regard Hamish as a prime physical specimen and nothing else. Talk about female chauvinism! I said crisply, 'Hamish is a lot more than a hunk. He's one of the nicest, kindest, most unselfish people I've ever met. And if he were my boyfriend – which as a matter of fact he's not – I'd count myself one of the luckiest.'

Roseanne raised an ironic eyebrow. 'Boy, you've got it badly!'

I didn't bother to deny it. But there was an interesting thought here that I was in no fit state to cope with just now, so for the moment I put it on 'hold'.

'Okay, everyone.' Edward, now holding a clip-board, had got to his feet. 'The bus will be outside in fifteen minutes to take us to the studios. Don't worry too much about your hair and make-up — ' Loud cheer from the boys – 'We'll take care of all that when we get there. Just fetch your things and be down in the hotel lobby by nine-thirty.'

'This is it,' Roseanne muttered beside me. 'Here we go, over the top.'

I struggled to my feet. My head felt as if it was stuffed with cotton wool and my body was one big ache. I'd never felt less like taking part in a TV quiz programme in my life.

Twelve

'Five minutes. Settle down, please, studio.'

We'd spent the morning in rehearsal, under boiling studio lights, and now we were ready to go. J.J. and I sat behind a desk marked 'Bradley'. Opposite were Roseanne and her partner, behind a desk marked 'Leeds'; and between us Sue Morrison, looking smaller in real life than she appeared on television. And out there, beyond the cameras, was the audience, now in a boisterously receptive mood after the comic's warm-up. I knew that somewhere among them were the Bradley supporters, including Julie and some of the other kids from school, but the lights were too dazzling for me to see them.

The floor manager gave the signal that recording had started. *Ignore the cameras*, we'd been told. In fact they weren't as close as I'd expected, and the only way you could tell which camera was working was by the little red light that went on. But even then you couldn't be sure that you were the one being focussed on, so it was far less inhibiting if you forgot about them, as they said.

Sue Morrison started off by introducing the teams, first us and then Leeds. 'From Bradley,' she said, 'we have Harriet Bowles and Jeremy

Dexter. Harriet, you're at Bradley High School, I believe?'

'Yes,' I said. Scintillating repartee, this.

'And what do you hope to do when you leave?'

Same old question. But, unlike last time, I had my answer ready. 'I'd like to be a dress designer.'

For a moment she looked surprised. Clearly this wasn't the answer she'd been briefed to expect. But she recovered quickly to say, 'It's easy to see you're interested in fashion. Tell me, did you design that very striking outfit you're wearing today?'

This was obviously my cue to launch into the old tablecloth routine. I embellished it a bit and the audience tittered appreciatively.

'Well, I'm sure we all wish you every success.' She passed on to J.J., who solemnly trotted out his ambition to be a research chemist, and then she moved swiftly on to the Leeds team.

'Right, now we've introduced the teams and you know the rules, so without any more ado let's begin the challenge!' Quick burst of jangly signature tune. 'Harriet, you have first choice. What's it to be?'

I looked up at the flashing lights on the display board. 'Literature, please.'

It should have been a doddle. Under normal circumstances I could have answered seventy per cent of the questions, no problem. But somehow the unreality of the situation had got to me – the lights, the heat, lack of sleep, above all the worry about Dad – and my brain seemed to go into reverse. I said Thackeray had written *Barchester*

Towers and couldn't remember the name of the main character in *Catcher in the Rye* (Holden Caulfield). Apart from that, I didn't do too badly. I scored eight points. But it should have been at least fourteen and I knew it.

J.J. chose Science and scored fifteen. At the end of the first round we were one point ahead of Leeds.

Next came the quickfire round of general knowledge questions. I made an effort to pull myself together, knowing this was where I had to be on top form because it was no use relying on J.J. But although I tried my hardest Roseanne and her partner were quicker on the buzzer. Leeds pulled ahead 33–31.

In the final specialist round Leeds had first pick, but it didn't really matter because the categories had changed. I was left with a choice between Nature and Sport, so I took Nature as the lesser of two evils. The questions were fiendish, such as 'Name one insect that belongs to the lepidoptera family'. When I guessed wildly at 'beetles' J.J. made an impatient sound beside me. Apparently I should have said moths or butterflies. My score was a miserable five. J.J. chose Current Affairs and scored eight.

By the last quickfire round I'd pretty well given up, so of course I did better, but by then it was too late. Leeds had won, by 52–45.

'And that ends another edition of Youth Challenge,' Sue Morrison said. 'We look forward to seeing Leeds again in the next round, but to Bradley we have – regretfully – to say goodbye.

Thanks for coming, Harriet and Jeremy. I hope you enjoyed yourselves?'

I put on a sickly smile and tried to look as if I'd had a ball. J.J. didn't even try.

'Anyway, you don't go away empty handed. You both take back with you a Challenger T-shirt and pen.' Sue Morrison turned directly to camera. 'So now it's goodbye. Thanks for watching. See you again soon.'

Waves from contestants. Cheers from studio audience. Final burst of signature tune. The floor manager signals: *Keep applause going*. Then: *Okay, you can stop now*.

'Well done, everyone. That was great. Just keep your seats while we check the recording . . . '

It was over.

'Who wants a lousy T-shirt anyway,' J.J. said disgustedly. 'I wouldn't be seen dead in one. What a ludicrous waste of time!'

I said feebly, 'We did our best.'

'I certainly did. I'm not so sure about you.'

I stared at him, wondering how on earth I could ever have thought he was so marvellous. Mean down-turned mouth, small piggy eyes . . .

'Everyone knows it was Trollope who wrote *Barchester Towers*,' he went on. 'And how you managed to make such a hash of those Nature questions is beyond me. They weren't all that difficult.'

'You didn't do so brilliantly yourself,' I pointed out. 'You hadn't a clue who's the present Minister of Transport.'

He gave me a frosty look. 'I might have done

considerably better if your father hadn't slammed his car into a tree last night.'

I was speechless.

He got up from his seat. 'I'm going to find the canteen. I need some coffee.' He went without bothering to ask if I'd like one too.

As I pushed back my chair Sandra Wymark appeared. 'Bad luck, Harriet. I'm sorry we shan't be seeing you again.'

'I'm sorry too,' I said.

'On reflection I think perhaps we were wrong to let you go ahead today. It was too soon after the crash. I'm sure you must still be feeling groggy.'

'Did it show? I tried not to let it.'

'No, you were fine. But not quite so bubbly as you were at the audition.' She smiled at me as we walked across the studio floor, taking care to step over camera cables. 'Your personality knocked Perry and I out that day. We couldn't wait to get you on the show.'

'Really?' I found this hard to believe. 'I thought I'd made a complete pig's ear of the whole thing.'

'Far from it. It's always personality that's the deciding factor, you know. Brains aren't as important as you might think.' Someone yelled at her and she said quickly, 'I'll have to go. With four shows to be recorded today we don't have much turn-around. Will you be okay?'

I nodded. 'My family's here somewhere . . . '

'That's good. Take care of yourself, Harriet. And the best of luck with your career. I hope I get a chance to buy one of your exclusive designs one day.'

137

'So do I. Thanks, Sandra.' When she'd gone I looked around vaguely for a familiar face. The first person I saw was Roseanne, so I congratulated her on winning and asked if she knew where the Bradley supporters were.

'No idea,' she said. 'I've just seen your gorgeous boyfriend, though. But then you can hardly miss him, can you?'

'You'd be surprised,' I said, thinking how easily I'd managed to miss Hamish even though he'd been right under my nose, figuratively speaking, for the last few months. I must have been blind, as Julie said. Or incredibly dim. 'Where is he?'

'Over there, by the door.'

She was right, he did stand out, being at least half a head taller than the rest of the Bradley crowd. Julie was next to him, with Harvey Feldman and Steve Harris and about ten others from school. I thanked Roseanne and wished her luck for the next round before going over to join them.

Tom Byford was the first to greet me. 'Well done, Harriet! You put up a marvellous show, considering what happened yesterday. How do you feel?'

'Fine,' I assured him. I wished people would stop asking me how I felt. Now that the show was over I was aware of my aching shoulders again and had a slightly sick sensation in the pit of my stomach. I stood there in a daze while Steve Harris clipped me matily on the shoulder and said, 'You were great, Owl,' and Julie murmured in my ear, 'You looked terrific in close-up. I was watching on one

138

of the monitors above our heads. But I didn't know you wanted to be a dress designer?'

'Neither did I,' I said. 'It's true, though. Once I'd thought of it I realised it was exactly what I wanted to do.'

'But how do you become one? It can't be all that easy.'

'Go to art college, I suppose. Study fashion and learn how to do it properly. I don't mind how hard I work.'

She squeezed my arm. 'Imagine! And all because we decided to make you a dress for the dance. You never know how things are going to turn out, do you?'

'You certainly don't.' I agreed, glancing across at Hamish. He was the one person I really wanted to be with, but we were separated by all these people who seemed to be treating me like some kind of celebrity, even though I'd lost.

Eventually I managed to edge my way over to him. 'Is Mum still at the hospital?' I asked.

He nodded. 'She decided to stay with your father, so I said I'd take you and Rupert over there by taxi as soon as the show was over.'

'Where's Rupert now?'

'Getting Sue Morrison's autograph.'

I looked where he was pointing and saw Rupert deep in conversation with one of his tele-idols. 'Gosh, we'd better rescue her! She's got to do another recording in a minute.'

'Don't worry, she'll soon send him packing when she's had enough. Where's J.J.?'

'Gone to the canteen.'

'I've arranged for him to travel back with the others on the coach. When can you be ready to leave?'

'As soon as I've said goodbye.'

'Okay. I'd better find J.J. and let him know what's happening.'

Now, to an outsider this may have sounded a fairly crisp, impersonal exchange. But it wasn't really impersonal. There was a lot we hadn't said, because we didn't need to. I could tell from the look in his eyes that he already knew my feelings towards him had changed; and the smile he gave me before he went was full of Highland promise.

By the time we reached the hospital I was feeling so happy that Dad totally misread the broad grin on my face and said, 'You won! I knew you would.'

'No, she lost,' Rupert said. 'But we had a fantastic time.'

We drew up some chairs around Dad's bed and for the first few minutes everyone talked at once. Then Mum said, 'Harriet, you tell us what happened.'

I gave them an edited run-down on the day's events. Dad listened with interest. Apart from the cut on his forehead and having his leg in plaster he looked completely normal, much to my relief. But when I admitted what a hash I'd made of the Nature questions he groaned and said, 'It's all my fault. If we hadn't broken down I might have been driving more slowly and then we wouldn't have skidded — '

'That's enough of that,' Mum interrupted. 'I

thought we'd agreed, no breast-beating. After all, it was only a quiz. The way you've been carrying on you'd have thought Harriet's entire future depended on it.'

In a way it had, I thought, catching Hamish's eye.

'Okay, okay,' Dad threw up his hands in mock-surrender. 'But you can't blame me for being furious I missed it. My daughter a star on television – and me stuck in a hospital bed with my leg in plaster.'

'You only missed the recording,' I pointed out. 'The actual programme won't be on telly for months. So you'll still be able to see it.'

Dad brightened. 'So I will.'

'Mind you,' I added, 'I don't think I shall be watching. I couldn't bear to see myself making those stupid mistakes all over again. I must have looked a right nana.'

'Not half such a nana as J.J. Dexter,' Rupert said. 'He didn't even know who the Minister of Transport was. If you ask me, he isn't nearly so intelligent as everyone tries to make out.'

Mum said, 'Intelligence can take different forms. Speaking for myself, I'd sooner have good old-fashioned commonsense any day of the week.'

'So would I,' I agreed fervently.

Again I caught Hamish's eye. I couldn't wait to be alone with him. We'd held hands in the taxi, but hadn't been able to say much because of Rupert. Mind you, talking didn't seem all that important any more. I seemed to have spent too much of my life talking my way in and out of things. Now I was happy to be silent – as long as I could be silent with Hamish.

Five months later we were all sitting tensely in front of the TV, waiting for 'Youth Challenge'. Half of me didn't want to watch it, but the other half couldn't bear not to. The sound of that familiar, jangly signature tune sent my stomach diving into my trainers.

'I'm going to hate every minute of this,' I muttered to Hamish, who was beside me on the sofa.

He put a comforting arm around my shoulders. 'Don't look if you don't want to. Just listen.'

But I had to look. Call it masochism, but I felt compelled to.

The first sight of the teams was in longshot. I couldn't even make out which was which. Then, while Sue Morrison made the introductions, the camera moved in closer and there was this crazy-looking girl, all mouth and glasses, saying she wanted to be a dress designer.

I groaned. 'That can't be me!'

'It's you all right,' Rupert said. 'Now you know what the rest of us have to put up with.'

'Ssssh!' hissed Mum and Dad, in unison.

Next the camera moved to J.J. He looked more ferret-like than ever and when he spoke his voice sounded high-pitched and pedantic.

'What a prat!' said Rupert.

'Ssssh!'

Rupert was right, though. J.J. didn't come over well. When he answered his specialist questions he looked smug if he got them right and furious if he was wrong. Watching him, I wondered how I could ever have deluded myself that I was in love with him. I must have been out of my head.

Hamish, reading my thoughts – he'd become even better at that in the last few months – pressed my shoulder closer against his chest. I responded with an answering pressure, but my eyes remained riveted to the screen.

She was a stranger, that girl with the glasses. I quite liked her. She had a nice smile. But she was far too eager, leaping in with both feet where she should have taken time to reflect. The jazzy top she was wearing looked good, although a little crudely put together. I'd learned a lot since then – in more ways than one.

When the programme was over Dad leaned forward to switch off, but Rupert stopped him. 'It's a cartoon next,' he protested. 'Bugs Bunny.'

So much for my moment of fame!